Praise for *The Goddess Chronicle*

"Fans of Kirino's crime novels will find much to savor in *The Goddess Chronicle*. . . . Kirino is a master at creating an atmosphere of unease and distrust between her characters. In her skillful hands we see that the divide between man and woman is greater than the one between humans and gods. Kirino's retelling is a taut, disturbing and timeless tale, filled with rage and pathos for the battles that women have to fight every day, battles which have, apparently, existed from the moment of creation."   —Tan Twan Eng, *The Guardian*

"Kirino wows with her latest novel . . . [her] elegant writing brings Namima—a tragic, sympathetic heroine—to vivid life. Readers will devour this tragic story and be left transformed."
                                                              —*Publishers Weekly*

"The central narrative is lyrical, with an impelling storyline that demands attention . . . This is a compelling tale, with foundations in an allegory-rich fable that more than deserves its rejuvenation."
                                                              —*The Independent*

"Kirino captures the rivalry-laced love of sisters, the bitterness of the female role in mythology and the destructive powers of yearning for vengeance."   —Shelf Awareness

"[*The Goddess Chronicle*] will make you think. There is a feel of the oral tradition of storytelling in this book that makes it seem like a story handed down from the older generation rather than a novel. One can almost imagine sitting with their grandmother and listening to this story and then passing it along to children of the next generation when the time comes. It is a feminist work in that it stars strong women in the lead roles and explores the roles of gender, but it is much more than that as well. It is a story of love and betrayal and then love once again. . . . A very good book that should be read and enjoyed by everyone."   —*Minneapolis Examiner*

THE GODDESS CHRONICLE

Also by Natsuo Kirino

Out
Grotesque
Real World
What Remains

THE GODDESS CHRONICLE

Natsuo Kirino

Translated from the Japanese
by Rebecca Copeland

CANONGATE
Edinburgh · London · New York · Melbourne

First published in Japanese as *Joshinki* in 2008 by Kadokawa Shoten
Publishing Co. Ltd

First published in Great Britain in 2012 by Canongate Books Ltd.,
Edinburgh, Scotland

Printed in the United States of America

ISBN: 978-0-8021-2110-3

Canongate
an imprint of Grove/Atlantic, Inc.
154 West 14th Street
New York, NY 10011

Distributed by Publishers Group West

www.groveatlantic.com

14 15 16 17   10 9 8 7 6 5 4 3 2 1

Myths are universal and timeless stories that reflect and shape our lives – they explore our desires, our fears, our longings, and provide narratives that remind us what it means to be human. *The Myths* series brings together some of the world's finest writers, each of whom has retold a myth in a contemporary and memorable way. Authors in the series include: Alai, Niccolò Ammaniti, Karen Armstrong, Margaret Atwood, A.S. Byatt, Michel Faber, David Grossman, Milton Hatoum, Natsuo Kirino, Alexander McCall Smith, Klas Östergren, Victor Pelevin, Ali Smith, Su Tong, Dubravka Ugrešić, Salley Vickers and Jeanette Winterson.

TODAY, THIS VERY DAY

1

My name is Namima – 'Woman-Amid-the-Waves'. I am a *miko*. Born on an island far, far to the south, I was barely sixteen when I died. Now I make my home among the dead, here in this realm of darkness. How did this come to pass? And how am I now able to utter words such as these? It is all because of the goddess: it is her will, nothing less. How strange it must seem, but the emotions I have now are much sharper than they ever were when I was alive. The words I speak, the phrases I weave together, are born from the very emotions I embody.

This tale may be spun from my words but I speak for the goddess, the one who governs the Realm of the Dead. My words may be dyed red with anger; they may tremble in yearning after the living; but they are all, each and every one, spoken to express the sentiments of the goddess. As will become clear later, I am a priestess – a *miko* – and like the famous reciter of old, Hieda no Are, who entertains the goddess with ancient tales from the age of the gods, I too serve her with all my heart.

The goddess I serve is named Izanami. I've been told that *iza* means 'well, then' and suggests an invitation; *mi* is 'woman'. She is 'the woman who invites'. Her husband's name is Izanaki: *ki* translates as 'man'. Izanami is the woman among women; she is all women. It would not be an overstatement to say that the fate she suffered is the fate that all the women of this land must bear.

Let me begin this tale of Izanami. But before I can speak of her, I must tell you my own story. I will start with my strange little life, brief as it was, and relate how I came to serve in Izanami's realm.

I was born on a tiny island in the easternmost reach of an archipelago, far to the south of the great land of Yamato. My island was so far south, it took one of our little boats almost half a year to row there from Yamato. And it was so far to the east, it was closer than all the rest to the rising of the sun in the morning, and by the same token to its setting in the evening. For that reason, it was believed that it was upon our island that the gods first set foot on land. It was small but sacred, and revered from ancient times.

Yamato is the large island to the north, and in time the other islands in the surrounding seas fell under its control.

But when I was alive the islands were still ruled by the ancient gods. Those we revered were our great ancestors. They sustained our lives; the waves and wind, the sand and stones. We respected the grandeur of nature. Our gods did not come to us in any specific form, but we held them in our hearts and understood them in our own way.

When I was a little girl, the god I usually pictured in my imagination was a graceful woman. Occasionally she would grow angry and cause terrible storms, but for the most part she provided for us with the fruits of the sea and the land. She was a compassionate goddess, protecting our men when they set out for the distant seas to fish. Perhaps my image of this goddess was influenced by the austere dignity of my grandmother, Mikura-sama. I will speak more of Mikura-sama in good time.

The shape of our island is unusual, resembling a teardrop. The northern cape is pointed and sharp, like the end of a spear, with dangerous crags jutting into the sea. Closer to the coast the terrain is gentle, sloping to a flat shoreline that wraps softly round the island. Along the southern end the land is nearly level with the sea. Whenever a tsunami blows ashore, that area swells with water. The island is so small that a woman or even a young child could walk its entirety in less than half a day.

Countless pretty beaches grace the south. Over time

the pounding waves beat the coral reefs into fine pure white sand, which glitters when the sun strikes it. The seas are blue, the sand white, and all along the coast yellow hibiscus grow rampant. The fragrance of the midnight peach scents the sea breezes. I cannot imagine anywhere else on earth as beautiful as the beaches of my island. The men would set sail from these beaches to fish and trade and would not return for close to half a year. In times when the fishing was not good, they'd press on to more distant islands to trade and would be gone for more than a year.

Our men caught sea serpents off our shores, gathered the shells from our beaches, and carried them to islands further south where they traded them for woven goods, strange fruits and, on rare occasions, rice. Their trading done, they would turn their boats and sail home. As a child I enjoyed those homecomings. My elder sister and I would run to the beach every day and eagerly look out to sea, hoping to be the first to catch sight of our father and older brothers returning.

The southern side of our island was thick with tropical trees and flowers, the life there so abundant the wonder of it could take your breath away. The roots of the banyan trees twisted and coiled across the sandy soil. Large camellias and the fronds of the fan palm blocked the rays of the sun. And broadleaf plantains grew in clusters where natural spring water bubbled up in pools. Life on the island was poor – food was scarce – but the flowers bloomed in such profusion that our surroundings were exquisite. White trumpet lilies grew along the steep cliffs, along with the hibiscus – which changed hue as the sun set – and purple morning glories.

The northern side of the island, with its cape, was quite different. Blessed with a rich loamy soil in which almost anything could grow, every inch of ground was covered with pandan thickets. The thorny spines on the leaves were so sharp it was impossible to walk through them. There wasn't a single road through the region, and passage to the cape from the beach was impossible. The sea on the northern side was not like that of the south, with its beautiful beaches: it was treacherous – deep, with swift-flowing currents. The waves that beat against the cliffs were rough. Only a god could land on the island in the north, of that there was no doubt.

But there was one way in. There was a sliver of path between the pandan trees just wide enough for an adult to pass. If more than one should travel there, they had to walk in single file. The path was thought to link the south to the northern cape. But none of us was allowed to test it. Only one person was meant to walk that path, and that was the high priestess, the Oracle. The northern cape was sacred ground: it was where the gods came, on their visits to our island, and where they left.

A huge black boulder marked the entrance to the path and stood as a reminder to those of us who lived clustered together on the southern shores that we were forbidden to enter the sacred ground to the north. We called the boulder 'The Warning'. Other stone slabs had been erected beneath the boulder and formed a small altar where we held our sacred rites. The path that opened behind the boulder was dark, even at midday, and during the rituals that were performed there, we children would be so shaken with fear if we caught sight of the yawning darkness that we'd turn on our heels and race home. We'd been told that the harshest punishment awaited any who dared go beyond The Warning. But more than the horrors we knew awaited us, it was the imagined ones that filled us most with fear.

There were other places on our island that were taboo, one to the east, the other to the west. They were sacred and only women who had come of age were allowed to set foot inside them. The Kyoido was on the eastern side of the island, the Amiido to the west. The Oracle lived just beneath the entrance to the small cape that jutted over the sea, and the Kyoido abutted her cottage. The

Amiido was in the precinct of the dead. Whenever anyone died, they were carried there.

As children we had heard that the Kyoido and the Amiido were tucked away in secret groves of pandans and banyans, where the growth fell back to form a circle. No one cut so much as a blade of grass there; the thickets naturally gave way to those circular openings. And within each sacred area a natural spring welled up into a pool – Kyoido means 'Pure Well' and Amiido 'Well of Darkness'. That is what I had been told, anyway, but I knew no more than that, except that they were forbidden to all but adult women. Only during funerals were men and small children allowed to enter.

I knew that when I came of age I would be allowed to enter. Part of me wanted to grow up quickly so that I could know what was hidden there, while another part felt an undertow of dread. I would stealthily peer through the brambles along the small dark paths that led to those secret spots, wondering. But I never tried to draw near the Amiido, where the dead were left. I found it far too frightening.

Our island has no particular name. We always referred to it simply as 'the island'. But when our menfolk were out on the seas, fishing, occasionally they'd come across men in other vessels who would ask them where they came from. It was their custom to respond, 'From Umihebi, the island of sea snakes.' I heard that as soon as they said as much the men on the other boats would lower their heads in a gesture of respect. Our island was known far and wide in the southern seas as the island where the gods came and went. Even the few people who lived on small, remote islands had heard of Umihebi.

The seas surrounding our island were abundant with snakes, hence our island's name. We called the snakes 'naganawa-sama'. In our dialect 'naganawa' means 'long rope'. They were lovely little creatures with yellow stripes running the length of their lithe black bodies. In the spring the naganawa-sama would gather in the caves beneath the seas to the south of our island to lay their eggs. The island girls would turn out in force, grab them, toss them into baskets and cart them back to special storehouses. But the naganawa-sama had a fierce will to live. Even after they'd been plucked from the seas and taken ashore, they would survive for close to two months. Once we were certain they were dead we would stretch them out along the beaches to dry. We used them to barter with those from other islands in exchange for precious foodstuffs. They were an excellent source of nutrition, and delicious, or so we heard. We never had a chance so much as to taste the delicacy ourselves.

Once when I was a little girl I crept into one of the storehouses to look at the *naganawa-sama*. Their eyes glittered brightly within the dark baskets. My mother told me that as they began slowly to dry out, the oil would ooze from their bodies and they would hiss horribly from the torment. It didn't occur to me at the time that we treated the snakes cruelly. Innocent of their suffering, I wanted to collect as many as I could to make my mother's life a little easier — she worked from sunrise to sunset — and I also wanted to offer up the snakes to my pious grandmother.

Collecting sea snakes was primarily woman's work. But that was not all the women of our island did. They tended the mountain goats and collected shellfish or seaweed from the shores. But the most important task that the women performed was prayer. They prayed for the safe return of the men fishing on the high seas. They prayed for the prosperity of the island. They prayed. And the great *miko*, the high priestess, the one known as the Oracle, was responsible for all the prayer rites.

The Oracle, Mikura-sama, was my grandmother. That meant I was born into the most prestigious family on the island. Mikura-sama was the only person on the whole island allowed to go beyond The Warning, the boulder, and enter the precincts of the northern cape. That was why my family was known as the Umihebi, the Clan of the Sea Snake. There was an island chief, who was charged with settling disputes and making laws, but my family had the privilege of producing the Oracle, generation after generation.

I might have been born into the household of the great *miko*, but I still enjoyed a carefree childhood. As a little girl, before I reached an age of understanding, my older sister, Kamikuu, and I played together, day in and day out. There were four children in my family. Besides Kamikuu, I had two brothers, but they were much older than we were. And because they were always fishing, I saw them so infrequently that at times I couldn't even remember what they looked like. On top of that, their father was not mine and Kamikuu's. I never felt close to my older brothers.

But Kamikuu and I were only a year apart and the best of friends. Once the men had taken to the seas, we were inseparable, as if bound to one another with rope. We'd run off to the cape beyond the Kyoido. Or we'd climb down to the lovely beaches where we'd trap crabs in the tide pools and play until the sun went down.

Kamikuu – her name meant Child of Gods – was a sturdy girl and the cleverest child on the island. Her skin was creamy white, her eyes round, and her features perfectly formed. She impressed all who saw her with her beauty. Quick-witted, compassionate and intelligent, she even had a lovely singing voice. She was just a year ahead of me, but no matter what we did, she was always better at it than I. I loved her more than anyone else in the world. I relied on her and followed her wherever she went.

I can't explain it well but gradually I sensed we were destined for different things. No, I really did. You see, the gaze others turned on Kamikuu was not quite the same as the one they turned on me. And when the men came back to the island after their fishing trips, they interacted with us differently. Everyone was particularly courteous with Kamikuu, treating her with great deference. When did I begin to notice this?

It was on her sixth birthday that the difference became crystal clear. All the men in the family – my father, uncles and brothers – made a special effort to return from fishing in time to join in with the celebration. The island chief, who had been bedridden for some time, took up his cane and came to our house. The celebration was wonderfully lively and lavish. Everyone on the island had been invited. Of course, not everyone could fit into our reception room so the overflow spilt into the garden. The guests brought dishes filled with treats I'd never seen before and set them on the woven mats my mother had spread out earlier. She and the other women in our family had worked ceaselessly for several days preparing food. They had butchered plenty of goats; there was sea-serpent egg soup, salted fish, and sashimi prepared from the kind of shellfish that can be found only on the deepest regions of the ocean floor. Star-fruit, mango, an alcoholic drink that smelt like fermented goat's milk, *sake* made from taro root, and rice cakes steamed with sun-dried cycad were squeezed on to the mats.

I was not allowed to attend the party, but Kamikuu sat in the seat of honour next to Mikura-sama, enjoying all kinds of treats. They were dressed in matching white ceremonial robes, their necks adorned with strands of pure white pearls. Normally Kamikuu and I ate together, and seeing her go had made me miserable. I felt as if she were being taken away from me, which made me terribly anxious. At long last the banqueting subsided and Kamikuu stepped out of the main house. I ran to her side. But Mikura-sama pushed me back.

'Namima, you are not supposed to be here. You are not to look at Kamikuu.'

'Why, Mikura-sama?'

'Because you are the impure one.'

As soon as Mikura-sama spoke, my father and the other men in the party stood up and planted themselves between me and Kamikuu.

'The impure one?' Her pronouncement stunned me. I hung my head, my whole body trembling. It wasn't long, though, before I felt someone's eyes upon me. When I looked up, Kamikuu was staring at me, her eyes filled with heart-wrenching pity. I drew back instinctively – she had never looked at me like that before. She turned to leave.

'Kamikuu, wait!'

I started to run after her but my mother and aunt grabbed my arms and held me back. My mother glared at me angrily. I knew, from the way everyone was behaving and because my face was tight with tears, that something was amiss, but no one paid me the slightest attention. I wanted to know what was going on. I didn't care that I'd already been shooed away. I slipped into the shadows cast by one of our outbuildings and kept a furtive eye on the events. Mikura-sama was leaving, leading Kamikuu away. All the islanders stood and watched as the two disappeared into the melting darkness. Nightfall on our island was as forlorn as a tiny ship alone on the great sea. My mother was watching from the kitchen. Beside myself with worry, I called to her over and over.

'Where are they going? Mother! Where is Mikura-sama taking Kamikuu? When will she come home?'

'For a walk,' Mother answered evasively. 'She'll be back before long.'

It was the deep of night. Of course they hadn't gone for a walk. They couldn't have got far – I could catch up to them if I tried. But when I started down the path, Mother took hold of me and would not let me go.

'You can't follow. Mikura-sama will not allow it.'

But why not? I didn't understand. I looked up at my mother, hoping she would explain why Kamikuu was allowed to go but I wasn't. 'Why? Why can't I?'

Mother stamped her foot and refused to let me past her. She also refused to offer any answers to my questions. But her eyes were filled with pity, the same kind of pity I had seen earlier in Kamikuu's. I could not make sense of it. Why, all of a sudden, were Kamikuu and I being forced apart? And why did it seem so final?

That was when I noticed all the food that had been left after the banquet. There were platters of goat meat that had not even been touched, along with fresh shellfish and slices of succulent fruit. Instinctively, I reached for some. But Mother gave my hand a sharp slap.

'You must never touch the food that Kamikuu has left. If you do you will be punished by the gods. That girl is to become Mikura-sama's successor.'

I stared up into my mother's face, shocked. I'd always assumed that my mother, Nisera, would become the next Oracle. She was Mikura-sama's daughter, after all. I knew

that our family had served as *miko* for generations and
that a member of my family would one day become
Mikura-sama's successor. But I had thought it would
happen far in the future. There was no mistaking what
Mother had said, though. Kamikuu was now in training
to replace Mikura-sama.

Mother went to throw away the leftover food. As soon
as she was gone I stepped outside and gazed up at the
stars. Where was Kamikuu now? What was she doing?
Even as I turned these questions over I felt another
weighing heavily in the corner of my heart. 'The impure
one'? What did it mean? It didn't surprise me that I had
not been selected to succeed Mikura-sama and become a
great Oracle. After all, Kamikuu was older. And she was
far better than I at everything. But how could Mikura-
sama look at me and know I was impure? What made me
impure? These questions nagged at me, and I was in such
turmoil I was unable to sleep that night.

The following morning Kamikuu came home. The
sun was already high in the sky, and the temperature,
too, had begun to rise. As soon as I saw my sister, I
ran out to greet her. The white festival robes she had
worn the night before were now lightly soiled, and she
looked exhausted. Hadn't she slept? Her eyes were
bloodshot and unfocused. Her feet and calves were

covered with nicks and cuts as though she'd run along the coral beach.

'Kamikuu! Where have you been? What happened to your feet?' I pointed to the cuts but Kamikuu merely shook her head.

'I'm not allowed to say. I'm not supposed to tell anyone where I went or what I did. Mikura-sama said so.'

I bet she took the path past The Warning, I thought. But had she gone all the way to the northern cape? Had she encountered any of the gods along the way? I could picture Mikura-sama carrying the pinewood torch, leading Kamikuu down the narrow road through the thicket of thorny pandan, their white garments glimmering faintly in the darkness. The vision was enough to make me tremble in fear.

Whatever Kamikuu had undergone that night made her seem distant – austere, even. I felt timid, uncertain as I looked at her. Mother came and pulled Kamikuu aside. I caught fragments of what she said.

'Didn't Mikura-sama tell you not to speak to Namima? She's impure. You will be defiled.'

Shocked, I turned to them but they had their backs to me and were not even aware that I was there. Tears rolled slowly down my cheeks. I was crouching as I listened, and I watched the teardrops splash onto my bare feet, white from the dust of the sand, and form slender streaks as they slid towards the ground. At that moment, even though I did not understand, I knew I was impure.

And so it came to pass that sisters who had been the best of friends were forced to follow separate paths. 'Separate' is not quite the right word. Our paths were more distinctly different, as if she were to follow the day and I the night; or she the inner road and I the outer; she to traverse the heavens and I the earth. That was the 'law' of the island – that was our 'destiny'. Of course, as a child, I had no way of understanding what it meant.

The following day Kamikuu gathered up her belongings and left the house. From now on she would live with Mikura-sama in her tiny cottage just beneath the entrance to the Kyoido cape. Because I had always believed Kamikuu and I would be together for ever, it hurt me to see her leave. I stood there and watched her move further and further away. I think she was sad to leave me, too. Whenever she could evade Mikura-sama's careful watch, she would turn back to me, her eyes full of tears.

Poor Kamikuu, 'Child of Gods'. It must have been even more difficult for her than it was for me. She was taken from her parents, from her brothers, from me, and from that day forward she was expected to train as the next Oracle. No longer would we play together on the beaches or run naked through the rain. No longer would we wile away our time collecting flowers and doing all the things children on our island were wont to do. The sweet days of childhood had ended so suddenly.

It wasn't long before the island chief gave me a new role to fulfil. My mother and the other women in the village took turns to prepare Kamikuu's meals. The chief told me that it would fall to me to deliver them to her. Apparently Mikura-sama had made her own preparations while she lived alone. But now, with another under her roof, my mother and others in the village had to prepare and deliver meals made especially for Kamikuu.

I carried the food to Kamikuu once a day; she divided it into two and ate it in two sittings. We used two baskets for this purpose, both carefully woven in tight plaits from the fronds of the betel palm, both with lids. Each day I carried one of the baskets laden with food and left it in front of Mikura-sama's cottage. Then I took up the empty basket, which had contained the meal from the previous evening, and carried it home to my mother.

My duty came with harsh restrictions. I must never lift the lid and look inside the basket. If Kamikuu had left any food in it, I was not to eat it but to carry the basket to the top of the cape on my way home and throw all of the contents over the cliff and into the sea below. Finally, I was never to speak to anyone of these matters. Those were the four rules I was given.

When I heard about my new assignment I was beside myself with joy. I now had an excuse to see Kamikuu and I would be able to learn more about her new life. What was Mikura-sama teaching her? How was she spending her days? I was bursting with curiosity.

The next day, as dusk set in, Mother handed me the basket. The weave was so tight, it was impossible to see what was inside. But as I carried it, the smells that wafted up from it were so intoxicatingly delicious I nearly grew dizzy. No doubt it contained a veritable feast. When Mother was preparing the food she had told me I wasn't allowed to watch so I had gone off to play. But from the way the contents now sloshed in their containers I guessed she had made a sea-turtle broth. Or perhaps sea-snake soup. And there was the smell of grilled fish, and the dried fish the men brought home after their long sea voyages. But even more precious was the handful of steamed rice I imagined to be inside the basket, wrapped neatly in a bamboo leaf.

Of course I had never tasted anything quite so delicious. I doubted that anyone else on our island would have eaten such delicacies. Far from it. Everyone was always hungry. The island was small and there was a limit to what we could grow. As it was, the island association was hard pressed to make the little we had go round. All it took was a heavy storm that damaged our crops and it wasn't unusual for some to starve to death. Sometimes a group of men went to sea and never came back because there was nothing for them on the island. I'm ashamed to admit it, but I couldn't help feeling envious that Kamikuu was allowed to eat such wonderful food.

Once Mother handed the basket to me, I carried it with the utmost care to the little cottage on the edge of the Kyoido grove. The road to Mikura-sama's house extended upward to the cape and I could hear the sound of the waves. I could also hear the murmur of Mikura-sama offering prayers. And just beneath her voice I heard Kamikuu's. I pricked up my ears to catch the words they chanted, humming in rhythm with them, not thinking about what I was doing.

For a thousand years, the northern cape,
For a hundred years, the southern beach,
A cord strung across the seas, calms the waves.
A net stretched across the mountains collects the winds.
Sanctify your song,
Rectify my dance.

Today, this very day,
May the gods
Live for ever.

'Is someone there?'

When I heard Mikura-sama's stern voice I shrank back. My grandmother opened the door and stepped outside. Her eyes narrowed into a momentary smile when she caught sight of me. I remembered how she had pronounced me 'impure' at the ceremony earlier, yet now she was gazing at me with the affection a grandmother bestows on a beloved grandchild. Relieved, I began to explain, 'Mikura-sama, the island chief told me I should bring this basket up here to you.'

As I handed it to her, I peered into the dimly lit cottage. Kamikuu was kneeling stiffly on the wooden floor. She glanced over her shoulder at me and smiled with delight, waving her tiny hand. I smiled, too, and waved back, but Mikura-sama quickly pulled the door shut.

'Namima, thank you for your trouble. When you come tomorrow, leave the basket in front of the door. Here's the basket from yesterday. Kamikuu didn't eat all the food so what she left is in here. Go up to the cape and throw the leftovers over the edge. And you mustn't sneak a bite for yourself. That, you must never, ever do.'

Basket in hand, I cut my way through the thickets of pandan and banyan. Hardy pemphis shrubs clung to the side of the cape as though climbing to the summit. I was so hungry that I was tempted to open the basket and steal a bite of the leftover food, but Mikura-sama's stern words rang in my ears. Once I reached the summit, I opened the basket and hurled the contents over the side of the cliff. Gingerly I worked my way to the edge and looked down. The morsels of food floated for a few seconds on the rolling waves, then sank.

It seemed so wasteful. But my mother and grand-mother had given strict instructions. The finest food the island could provide was to be gathered for Kamikuu and what she left was to be thrown away. I had no choice but to obey. And the task I'd been given had allowed me a glimpse of my sister. She had looked well so I was happy. I began to sing as I turned for home.

Little girls of my age rarely walked alone at night. As I hurried along the southern beach, the cliffs glittered white under the full moon. I could see the bats taking flight from under the droopy branches of the tea trees. Suddenly I was terrified, my eyes darting left and right. Tomorrow I would make this trip again, and the night after that, and after that as well. Would I ever grow used to it? How could I? The night scenes were so frightening.

The moon shone brightly over the beach, and I saw a person. Someone had come to meet me, perhaps, worried for my safety. I started to run but almost as soon as I did I froze. I didn't recognise the person: a woman, with long hair flowing down her back, wearing white. She was plump, her skin fair. 'Mikura-sama,' I called, but stopped. She was similar to my grandmother, but she was not Mikura-sama. The woman caught sight of me and smiled. With barely two hundred people on the island, how could there be someone I'd never seen before?

She must be a goddess. Overcome, I felt gooseflesh rise on my arms. My legs would not move. The woman turned and walked into the sea, disappearing into the darkness. I had met a goddess! I had met a goddess who had smiled at me with love. My heart surged with joy. I felt immense gratitude to the island chief and Mikura-sama for assigning to me this task. The goddess did not appear to me again, but my vision of her became my most precious secret. From that moment on I was able to endure the hardship of delivering Kamikuu's food.

And so I began the ritual of walking the path to the Kyoido cottage with the basket of food. I went every day without fail. Some days the summer sun beat down mercilessly; on others bitter winds swept in from the north.

There were days when I was buffeted by rain and on others there were sand storms. It didn't matter. I carried the basket to that roughly hewn door and brought away the basket that had been left there. The basket I took was filled with the most delectable food, and the basket I carried away was full of the food Kamikuu had left. No matter how delicious the feast, she seemed to eat hardly any of it. Still, I threw what remained over the edge of the cliff and hurried home. I knew that Mikura-sama was listening: she wanted to hear the food hit the surface of the water, making sure that I had thrown away what Kamikuu had left. I did as I was told, and I never looked inside the basket.

It seemed that Mikura-sama ate none of the delicacies herself, and I did not understand why. I wanted to ask my mother about it, but I was afraid to. I was 'impure'. And I was afraid there was some connection between the two.

A year passed before I caught another glimpse of Kamikuu. On the island we offer prayers on the thirteenth night of the eighth month for the safety of those who voyaged by sea. Mikura-sama conducted the ceremony, but this time, Kamikuu sat beside her before the altar. And she kept her eyes on Mikura-sama, watching carefully as she recited the prayers.

Heavens . . . we bow before you.
Seas . . . we bow before you.
Island . . . for you we pray.
Heaven-racing sun, revering you,
Sea-bed creeping sun, shunning you,
Our men sing the seven songs.
Our men spell the three verses upon the waves.
Heavens . . . we bow before you.
Seas . . . we bow before you.
Island . . . upon you we rely.

Finally, at Mikura-sama's urging Kamikuu stood up. She beat on a large white shell in rhythm with Mikura-sama's chanting. When I saw my sister I was astonished. She had grown so much taller. Her figure had filled out, and her skin was whiter than anyone's I had seen on the island, so finely grained it was lustrous. Kamikuu was beautiful.

I, on the other hand, had hardly changed. I was still dark-skinned and shabby. I was thin and small – no doubt because my diet was poor. On the rare occasions when I caught a small crab, I was delighted. Normal meals consisted of taro root, sago seeds, mugwort, fern fronds and other such greens, small fish, shellfish and seaweed. Plenty of edible plants grew on the island, but it took time to cultivate them. And if we gathered them all at once, they would soon be depleted. Mother and I had to go to the beach every morning to collect seaweed, shellfish, minnows and crabs.

On days when storms prevented us doing that, we didn't eat. But Kamikuu ate a magnificent feast all by herself, the like of which most people on the island could not even dream. No wonder she was beautiful. The sight of Kamikuu's rounded body overwhelmed me – I couldn't speak. We had been so close, yet the distance between us now was vast.

Mikura-sama's prayers ended. She set off towards her Kyoido cottage with Kamikuu, who stole a hurried glance in my direction and nodded. I forgot about the gulf between us. All I could think now, from the depth of my heart, was how much I wanted to talk to Kamikuu, to play with her again.

That evening I took the basket Mother handed to me, as I had done in evenings past. As usual I smelt a delicious aroma rising from it. But this time, I asked Mother, 'Why is it only Kamikuu who can eat such delicious food?'

Mother hesitated, then said, 'Because she is destined to become the next Oracle.'

'But Mikura-sama doesn't have food like this.'

'Mikura-sama doesn't need it any more.'

I had no idea what Mother was talking about.

'But isn't Mikura-sama still the great *miko*?'

Mother smiled. 'Mikura-sama is preparing the next *miko*. Her turn is almost over. What if something were to happen to Mikura-sama? Kamikuu must be ready to take over. In this way we can keep up the tradition. The one thing this island cannot allow is the loss of its Oracle.'

Mother peered inside the large earthenware jar to see how much water we had left. There had been little rain recently and she was worried. I looked inside the jar, too. Barely an inch remained. Soon we would be forbidden to drink it. We would have to save it for Kamikuu.

'Why aren't you the next great *miko*, Mother? You're Mikura-sama's daughter. Why did she choose Kamikuu?'

I assailed Mother with one question after another. She continued staring at the water in the jar and did not answer. When I peered into it I saw my face floating alongside hers. I stared hard at my mother's reflection. Her face was small and dark, exactly like my own.

'You're still a little girl. It's hard for you to understand, but on our island everything is already decided. *Yang* is always followed by *yin*. Mikura-sama is *yang*. That means her daughter is *yin*, and my daughter, Kamikuu, is *yang*.'

Mother stopped and looked away. I might have been just a little girl at the time but I knew what this meant.

'Then I'm *yin*?'

'Yes. And if you had a little sister she would be *yang*. *Yin* and *yang* are the dual forces of nature, like day and night, and they continue one after another for ever. Fate decrees it so. That means, of all the people on the island, Kamikuu must live long and bear children. One of her children must be a daughter, and that daughter must bear a daughter. That is the only way we can give birth to a great *miko* and continue the tradition. So, you see, it is our fate — we live so that the island can live. Or, really, I should say that the island lives by our fate. We carry the future of the island. We keep everyone going.'

I saw a smile spread across Mother's face in the water jar. Finally the riddle had been solved. Satisfied, I let out a sigh. For the sake of the island, Kamikuu had to eat rich food, live a long life and give birth to a daughter. I might have been young, but I felt profound pity for my elder sister and her heavy burden. I wondered if I could have borne the pressure. I decided I would do everything in my power to help her. And I began to wonder if the goddess I had seen on the beach that night had come to impress this obligation on me.

Of course, at the time I had no idea that I shouldered an entirely different burden.

2

Seven years had slipped past since Kamikuu had begun her training. She was now thirteen and I was twelve. I continued to carry food to her without fail even on stormy days or when I was burning with fever. And over that time, though the amount increased and the basket grew heavier, the contents never varied, or so it seemed to me. Even so, Kamikuu ate lightly – the days when she finished the food in the basket were so few that I could have counted them on one hand – but I honoured Mikura-sama's instructions and threw the leftovers into the sea. No matter how tempted I was to steal just a bite, I was so terrified of the consequences that I resisted.

I knew people on the island were starving, and it pained me to be so wasteful. I often felt frustrated with Kamikuu – if I had been her I would have eaten all that was given to me, regardless of whether I was hungry or not. That annoyance sank fast into my heart.

One night a strong damp wind blew long and hard across the island, drenching the trees. It was the kind of wind that the islanders believed foretold the arrival of an unseasonable storm. Whenever we had had great storms in the past, they had been preceded by just this kind of wind. It would suddenly abate, only to be followed by another gale and rain.

I watched the night sky nervously. The moon was covered with thick dark clouds, the sky jet black. Wisps of cloud sailed across the darkness, like shredded white flower petals. When I stopped to listen I could hear in the distance a rumbling noise, as if the seas were growling. It sounded as if the heavens were roiling with a furious strength that no human could ever match. I was terrified.

The slender noni stalks bent so low that I feared they would snap. If the wind grew much stronger it would destroy all the crops the islanders had struggled to plant, and I knew the women – the only ones left on the island now – would be working frantically: they would be binding stones and logs with rope then lashing them to their huts in an attempt to weigh them down against the gale. But more than anything they would be pre-occupied with worry over the men who were fishing. Of course, Mikura-sama would have sequestered herself in her shrine to pray diligently for their safe return and for the protection of the island. But over the ages our island had known many times when nature had defeated even the most fervent prayers.

My mother had told me that about fifteen years ago a strong wind had swept over the island just when the men were almost ashore. Many boats had capsized. The man who became my father was on one of them. He managed to swim ashore and was not harmed. But only ten or so young men were as lucky as he was. For years to come, there were no men older than the few who had swum ashore. That storm had taken the life of my brothers' father, my mother's first husband.

But Mikura-sama said that in exchange for Nisera's husband's death, the island gained Kamikuu, Child of Gods, and Namima, Woman-Amid-the-Waves, so we should rejoice. She gathered the islanders together and told them that to all things there is a good side and a bad. We must consider both, she said. We must overcome our sorrows and search for the good in all things.

Mikura-sama's philosophy held true for Kamikuu. She was taken from her family and forced to endure strict training in order to become the next Oracle. But she ate delicious food every day. Other islanders would starve but Kamikuu would survive.

What fate awaited me? I thought about this as I cradled the basket of Kamikuu's food, walking into the powerful wind. I was so slight I was afraid it might pick me up and carry me away. Yet I couldn't help noticing that the fragrance rising from the basket that evening was especially mouthwatering. I had had my supper some time ago, but my stomach protested at the scent from the basket. That day, Mother and I had eaten mugwort and seaweed. That was all. But we were grateful to have food, and enough of it. Old people who lived alone and the poor had nothing to eat. Mother told me she'd seen any number combing the beach, desperation on their faces as they searched the windswept sands.

Today the basket seemed to contain steamed rice cakes, a thick broth of steamed *naganawa-sama* and goat meat. Something was different, though. Mikura-sama had come to talk to Mother early this morning. Mother had called her female relatives together and they had set off towards The Warning, despite the wind, to gather kuiko fruits. They stain your fingertips bright red when you so much as touch them. When Kamikuu and I were little, we used to paint our nails with kuiko juice. I do not know why Mother needed the kuiko, but I felt certain that the meal inside the basket tonight was particularly special.

Of course, that was the least of my worries. The further up the path I walked, the stronger the wind grew. The houses along the way rattled and shook, their doors fastened tight. The palm fronds and noni stalks rustled noisily and swayed so wildly I was sure that some giant creature was writhing and thrashing just ahead of me. The path I was used to following seemed new tonight. Waves lashed the cliffs with a thunderous roar. The entire island was vibrating. It was just the kind of night, I convinced myself, when the gods landed on the northern cape to wander the island, revealing their wild and angry faces. I was so frightened, it was all I could do to keep walking.

I hurried to Mikura-sama's cottage. The basket that I had delivered yesterday was in front of the door, with a large piece of coral on top of it to stop it blowing away. I put down the basket I had brought and picked up the other. How strange, I thought. It felt as if none of the food had been touched.

'Is that you, Namima?'

The door opened and Mikura-sama peered out at me.

'Mikura-sama, is Kamikuu ill? The basket is just as heavy as it was when I brought it.' I pointed to the basket I had just picked up.

To my surprise, Mikura-sama grinned. 'We are well, Namima – and you have no need to worry about things that don't concern you. Remember your promise. Throw the leftovers away. Kamikuu has become a woman, that is all.'

Kamikuu's body was now ready to bear children. From now, her future was bright. But I was frightened. Kamikuu had entered a world beyond my reach. I wanted to talk to her, congratulate her. I lingered in front of the cottage. But Kamikuu did not come out. I had little choice but to turn back into the wind.

'Namima.'

A man's voice called my name from the darkness of the thickets. It startled me and I nearly dropped the basket. But no one was there. Just when I had convinced myself that I had been mistaken, I heard the voice again.

'Namima, wait.'

'Who is it?'

'I didn't mean to frighten you,' the man said. But he did not show himself to me. Most of the men were fishing, leaving only the elderly and the boys on the island. If a young man were left, he was too sick to fish. But this man's voice seemed young and strong. Who was it? I peered into the darkness.

'It's Mahito.'

Mahito of the Umigame family. The eldest son. He was sixteen and well past the age when he should have joined the fishing parties. But Mahito was forbidden to fish. I was confused. I didn't know what to do so I stared at my feet. According to the law of the island, we were not to speak to members of the Umigame – the Sea Turtle – family. But I knew Mahito. I had seen him alongside the women on the beach collecting seaweed. And for some unexplained reason the memory of his sunburnt face now made my heart pound. I couldn't ignore him. It must be humiliating for him to work alongside the women. Every time I glimpsed his dusky face on the beach, I found myself longing to help him with his quest for food. I wanted to take food to his family. That feeling now shot through my heart with such intensity that it hurt. I answered softly, 'Good evening, Mahito.'

He stepped from the shadows and appeared before me, relief on his face. I knew he had hidden from me because he was worried lest someone see me violating the island law.

'Namima, I'm sorry I frightened you but you must not be caught talking to me.'

Mahito was much taller than I. He had the sturdy build of a fisherman. But he always crouched and stooped, as if he did not want anyone to notice him.

'We must be careful,' he added. He looked cautiously around him. The Umigame family was under a curse, or so I had heard. They had been ostracised by the rest of the island community, a cruel and severe punishment. Normally when a boy came of age he set out with the other men to fish. But a boy from a family that was ostracised was not allowed to fish. That amounted to telling that family they must starve to death.

'I'm impure, too. People aren't supposed to talk to me, either.' I voiced what had troubled me for a long time. At Kamikuu's sixth birthday celebration, Mother and Mikura-sama had told me I was impure. They hadn't mentioned it since. But others on the island now refused to look at me. And they often refused to speak to me.

'Don't let it upset you.'

Now it was Mahito's turn to encourage me. We exchanged glances and smiled.

I sympathised secretly with Mahito's family: the Umigame was second only to the great *miko*'s, second, that was, to my family, the Umihebi. If for some reason the Umihebi family failed to produce a daughter, it was up to the Umigame to place one in line to become the next Oracle. But the Umigame had been able to produce nothing but boys. Seven sons, starting with Mahito. His mother had done her best to give birth to a daughter, desperate to continue the family lineage, but birth after birth, all were male. And almost all of the babies had died. Mahito and his two younger brothers, Nihito and Mihito, had been the only ones to survive.

'Is your mother well?' I asked.

Mahito's gaze was unwavering, the lines of his face strong and clean. He was the handsomest youth on the island. Had he been allowed to go out to fish, he would have been a success. His face softened when he heard my question, but he lowered his voice to answer.

'She's going to have another baby.'

I offered my congratulations hesitatingly.

'She is certain she will have a girl this time. But I'm not sure . . .'

Mahito let out a deep sigh. If his mother didn't produce a daughter, the curse on the family would not be lifted. He and his two brothers would have to live the rest of their days as outcasts. Their mother was now nearing forty. Pregnancy at her age was as dangerous as it was necessary.

'It will go well,' I offered hopefully. 'This time she will have a girl.'

'She must. But, Namima, that's why I'm here. I must ask for a favour.' Mahito seemed reluctant to continue. 'In the basket . . . You have Kamikuu's leavings in it.'

Instinctively I hid the basket behind my back. Both Mikura-sama and my mother had told me never to talk about the basket or its contents.

'You need not hide it,' Mahito continued. 'Everyone on the island knows.'

I looked up at him. His expression was grim.

'If there's a little left over would you let me have it instead of throwing it away? I want to give it to my mother. Without it, I'm afraid she'll die.'

I couldn't believe he'd asked such a thing. I didn't know what to do. 'But Mikura-sama—'

'I know,' Mahito interrupted. 'No one may touch whatever touches Kamikuu's lips. It's the island law. But my family will starve. My mother has given birth to four babies who died. She will soon give birth to her eighth. She's convinced it'll be a girl. But if she doesn't do something to build her strength the birth will kill her. That's why I've come to you, Namima. To beg for the leftovers. Please. I know I'll be cursed but I don't care.'

If I said no, would he take the food by force? I stared up at his face. His features were set. The whites of his eyes glittered in the darkness – with tears. I held out the basket to him. 'Just today.'

'Thank you – thank you. I am indebted to you.' Mahito lowered his head.

Suddenly I was seized with fear. I looked behind me. I thought I had heard footsteps, but it was only the wind in the trees. 'Wait! Give me the basket. Mikura-sama will be waiting to hear the leftover food hitting the water.

We must replace the food with something I can throw instead. Hurry.'

I spoke sharply. If I delayed much longer, I was afraid Mikura-sama would come out, wondering why she hadn't heard the customary sound.

Mahito sprang into action. No longer attempting to conceal himself, he darted along the path gathering the largest taro leaves he could find. I removed the basket lid and placed the leftover food on them. I saw that the steamed rice had been dyed red with the juice of the kuiko fruits. A celebratory dish. And hardly any had been touched. Startled, I nearly dropped the container of sea-snake broth. The thick liquid splashed over the rim onto our wrists and dribbled to the ground. The smell scented the air around us. I don't know how best to explain what I felt at that moment. Perhaps, for the first time, it was the sadness of knowing that the world had no place for me.

I saw Mahito's hands tremble. I understood that he was scared too, which calmed me. 'Please give this to your mother.'

Mahito wrapped the food in the broad leaves. He then took a handful of earth, wrapped it in another taro leaf and placed it in the empty basket for me. 'Thank you, Namima.'

He offered his thanks to me again, looking down regretfully at the puddle of broth on the ground before he stamped on it, covering it with earth.

When I saw him do this, I said, 'Mahito, if you come tomorrow at the same time I'll let you have more. But bring something to put the soup in.'

Again he whispered that he was indebted to me. With one more word of thanks he disappeared into the darkness towards his ramshackle hut on the edge of the village. Ours was a small community so we did what we could to help each other, building cottages and boats, mending fishing nets. But for the Umigame family there would be no neighbourly assistance. Every day for them was an ordeal.

I headed quickly towards the precipice. There, I turned the basket over and held it out above the cliff edge, letting the contents tumble into the waters below. The splash this time seemed to come a little sooner and sound louder than usual. The winds raged, but I was rooted to the spot, aghast at the depth of the sin I had committed. The outrage made me shudder with fear. I had disobeyed Mikura-sama's injunction – no, I had done worse: I had disobeyed the law of the island. But that law seemed unjust. When people were starving, what right had I to throw food away? It made no sense. In a tiny corner of my heart, I felt ennobled.

I started down the path to my house but turned as I did so to look behind me. I was startled to find someone standing there. Kamikuu.

'What are you doing? You frightened me almost to death!'

Kamikuu smiled. I hadn't seen her outside the cottage for such a long time. She was a head taller than me, well fleshed and beautiful.

'Why did you creep up behind me?'

I didn't know if she had seen me talking to Mahito or not. But Kamikuu smiled sweetly and said, 'The wind is so strong that I was worried. I wanted to be sure you hadn't fallen over the edge of the cliff.'

We had had many windy nights in the past. Why had she decided to look for me this evening? The evening when Mahito had appeared? I was suspicious. Was it really Kamikuu — or was it Mikura-sama in disguise? I stared at her, silent.

Puzzled, Kamikuu pressed me: 'Namima! What's wrong? I haven't seen you for so long – won't you at least greet me?'

That was when I saw her dimple, the dimple I remembered from when we were little. It was Kamikuu. I sighed with relief as I thanked her for her concern. But I still felt awkward and I must have seemed too formal.

'I'm not a stranger!' she said. She pulled an adult face and looked at me with disappointment.

Now that she had become a woman, she would soon be assigned a husband and then she would have to produce babies until she gave birth to a daughter. Just like Mahito's mother.

'I didn't mean to be unfriendly!'

Kamikuu came up to me and placed her soft, plump hands on my shoulders. 'It's been so long, Namima. I've missed you.'

'And I've missed you.'

Even as I said this, my heart was pounding. If Kamikuu had seen me giving Mahito food, what could I do? If she told Mikura-sama what she'd seen, both Mahito and I would be punished. I would probably be exiled from the island along with Mahito's family. We'd be sent out to sea on a rickety boat in the dead of winter, just as a fierce storm approached. That was what happened to exiles. They did their best to stay afloat, but within a matter of days the boat would return to the island empty. But surely Kamikuu loved me too much to get me into trouble – didn't she? I stood there petrified.

Before I could speak, she tugged my sleeve to her nose and sniffed. 'What's this? I smell broth.'

I cocked my head to the side and feigned innocence.

'I must have spilt some on my hand when I tossed the food over the cliff.'

'Of course. Namima, with each sip of soup I take, I think of you and wish I could share my food with you. I leave each meal half eaten, wishing you could have the rest.'

Kamikuu spoke so apologetically that tears rose to my eyes. It was too late. Kamikuu had now entered adulthood and she belonged to a world far beyond my reach. But tonight I had stepped into a world further still from the one she shared with Mikura-sama. Mahito and I had defied the law of the island. I looked up at my sister and said, 'Kamikuu, Mikura-sama told me that you are a woman now. Congratulations.'

'Thank you.' Kamikuu's response was lacklustre. Then, out of the blue, she asked, 'Have you seen Mahito? Is he well?'

Panic shot through me. Kamikuu had seen me handing Mahito the food, hadn't she?

'I haven't seen him for some time, so I can't say. Why do you ask?' My voice quivered with the lie but I wanted to know what lay behind Kamikuu's question. Was she planning to tell Mikura-sama what Mahito and I had done? Or would she prove to be an ally?

'Namima, I must tell you a secret. I can't tell anyone

else.' She looked around her. 'It's true that I have become a woman, and I shall soon begin to have babies. That is my fate. If I could have a baby with a man like Mahito, I would be happy. But Mikura-sama told me I can't, so long as Mahito's family is under a curse.'

I had no idea what to say in response. Uneasy, I gazed at the ground. Kamikuu grabbed my hand. 'Namima, it would be terrible to have a baby with a man you disliked.'

After a while, I nodded.

Kamikuu misunderstood. 'Forgive me, Namima. I didn't mean to talk about this. It's just that I have no one to talk to except Mikura-sama. I wanted to share my feelings with you. Please don't let it worry you.'

'No, no. It's all right. Thank you for telling me.'

Had Kamikuu seen me with Mahito? Was this her way of warning me to keep away from him? Or did she truly want to unburden herself to me? I couldn't tell.

She gave my hand a gentle squeeze. 'I shall see you later. If I don't hurry back now Mikura-sama will be angry. Be careful going home – the wind is strong enough to blow you away.'

Kamikuu turned towards Mikura-sama's cottage and went back down the path through the forest. The warmth of her grip on my hand lingered and her words, too, remained with me. *If I could have a baby with a man like*

Mahito . . . Kamikuu was in love with him. Perhaps that was why she had pretended not to see me handing him the food. Or had she come to share her feelings with me, as she had said? Oh, if that were true, how happy it would make me. But if it were not, she had come to make sure that I didn't grow close to Mahito. I had no idea what to think.

Later, a day would come when it was made clear to me that Kamikuu had the power and the right to stand between Mahito and me – if she so chose.

The next day a terrible storm swept across the island, bringing with it torrential rains and gales. The battering was merciless. And still I had to carry food to Kamikuu. Mother covered me with banana leaves to keep out the rain and held them in place with strong rope. She wrapped it around me, coil after coil, but even that was not enough to withstand the wind: it tore away one leaf, then another and another. By the time I had fought my way to Mikura-sama's cottage, I was soaked to the bone. The basket I had delivered last night was under the eaves. When I lifted it, I found it still as heavy as when I had left it. Normally that would have depressed me but today all I could think was how happy Mahito would be, and my heart lifted in joy. As I exchanged the baskets, I heard Kamikuu's voice on the other side of the door.

'Namima, be careful on your way home. The wind is so strong. Mikura-sama has gone to the altar to pray.'

The altar was in the centre of the Kyoido sacred grove. Mikura-sama must have gone there to pray for the safety of the men fishing on the high seas. And Kamikuu had gone out of her way to make sure I knew she was there – because she knew I would meet Mahito? I was gripped by doubt, but I believed that Kamikuu was my ally. Surely she wasn't my enemy. I had no proof, of course: it was just that I could not get out of my mind the memory of the trust and affection we had shared as sisters.

I made my way quickly through the pandan thickets, alert for falling thorny branches. Mahito was waiting in the same place as he had been the night before, dripping wet. He'd also covered himself with banana leaves, which had provided little protection.

'Namima, I wish you did not have to come out on a day like this.'

His concern, though kind, made me nervous. 'Mahito, hurry. The food is getting wet.' I was shivering with cold and could hardly speak.

Mahito slipped something wrapped in moon laurel leaves into my basket.

'What's that?'

'Sand.'

I handed him the food in exchange. As I started to walk away, he gripped my arm.

'Wait. The winds on the cape are too strong. Let me do it.'

'I can't. Mikura-sama is at the altar. She might see.'

'I don't care. If you die, Namima, I have nothing. They can exile me, sentence me to death . . . I don't care.'

No one had ever said anything like that to me before. I was stunned and stood rooted to the spot. Mahito yanked the basket from my hands and dashed towards the cape. The rain was torrential and the wind so strong that only a powerful man like Mahito could have neared the cliff safely. As soon as he had thrown away the contents of the basket, he hurried back to me. 'Namima, light as you are, the wind would have carried you over the edge.'

Even if it had, the island elders would have found someone else to carry Kamikuu's food. That was the law. And I had broken it. I had betrayed Mikura-sama by giving Mahito food. I had taken his bundle of sand in place of the food I had stolen, and he had thrown it into the sea on my behalf. And even if Kamikuu didn't say a word to Mikura-sama, she would know what I had done.

Wouldn't she? I would be punished. What would they do to me? The more I thought about it, the more terrified I became. I trembled with fear.

'What is it?'

The branches of the banyan under which Mahito was standing waved violently in the wind.

'I'm afraid of being punished.'

Mahito pulled me suddenly into his arms and whispered hoarsely, 'No one will touch you. I will protect you!' But his voice quivered.

We were soaked and trembling in each other's arms. Our sin had terrified us and we clung together for reassurance. Yet I was giddy over the bond we shared. I was in love with Mahito.

'I'll walk back with you.' Mahito led me by the hand as he cradled the empty basket. Twigs and pebbles blew against us as we walked. Down by the sea the wind carried the spray from the waves into the air. We were so wet we looked as if we'd been washed ashore. We struggled on, step by step.

'How is your mother?' I shouted into Mahito's ear. The roar of the wind was so loud that we had to shout to be heard. I could see my house now just ahead.

Mahito's voice darkened. 'She won't even try to eat. She asked me where I had found such fine food, but I was sure she knew. She started to cry, thinking about the punishment that lay in store for me.'

'And today?'

'Well, she must eat. If she doesn't she will die. And if she dies there'll be no reason for the elders to keep me, my brothers and our father alive. The island would have no use for us. We will all die if she dies . . . Namima, I shall see you tomorrow.'

And with that Mahito turned quickly towards his home. I had never before encountered anyone with such strength. The rest of us lived such timid lives, fettered by laws, fearful of breaking them.

Tomorrow! I shall see Mahito tomorrow! Already I was looking forward eagerly to the day ahead. The promise of seeing his face just one more time made me feel life was worth living. For the first time ever, my heart danced with delight.

We met every night. I gave him the food left in the basket, and he gave me a substitute to toss over the cliff into the sea. Then we would share the dark path back to the village, lost in conversation. Needless to say, we were careful to avoid being seen.

Mahito's mother delivered her eighth child. Another

boy. He, too, died shortly after birth. Everyone on the island was more certain than ever that the Clan of the Sea Turtle was cursed. The day after his tiny brother's death, Mahito failed to appear. I threw the food over the edge of the cliff and walked home alone. It had been some time since I had thrown it away, and once again I was struck by how wasteful it was.

On the third night after the baby's death, Mahito was waiting for me in the thicket by the path. The moon was full and in the light it cast I could see how gaunt his face had grown. His clothing was in disarray, and his long hair, which was normally bound back neatly with thin reed stalks, fell in loose tangles over his shoulders. My heart ached for him, as he drew closer to me.

'Mahito, where have you been these last three days?

'Attending the funeral at the Amiido.'

'How is your mother?'

'She blames herself. She thinks it's her fault for not eating the food I brought for her. And she swears that next time she'll eat everything she can for the sake of the baby and so that the rest of us can continue to live on the island.'

'Next time?'

'The next time she is pregnant.'

I could tell it was difficult for Mahito to talk about

this. His mother's health would suffer from all these pregnancies, one after another. I held out the basket, which was full, just as it had been on the past nights. 'What should we do with the food?'

Mahito was quiet, sunk in his thoughts. I had detained him longer than usual with conversation, and on such a night, sound carried far. Mahito looked around cautiously, afraid that someone might have followed us. Just to think of what might happen if we were caught brought tears to his eyes. He peered hard into the darkness, the tears glittering when they caught the moonlight.

'Namima, let's eat it. Let's break the law together so we can live.'

Startled by Mahito's words, I stared up at him. He pulled the basket from my arm and tore off the lid. When I looked in I could see it was just as Kamikuu had said it would be. She had left exactly half of everything. She had left half of the goat-meat dish, half of the bowl of sea-turtle broth, and half of the fish. Kamikuu had said, 'I want to give it to you.' She must have known that I was giving whatever she left to Mahito to help his family. I wanted to tell Mahito what I thought, but I hesitated because of what else Kamikuu had said. She had said she wanted to have Mahito's baby. That was when I realised I was jealous of Kamikuu's power.

'Namima, eat.'

Mahito stuffed some goat meat into my mouth. Then he took a piece for himself. A strange taste filled my mouth. I was too horrified by the crime I was committing to judge whether that taste was good or bad. I was sure it was the same for Mahito. We kept our eyes locked on one another as we ate, and before we knew it the sumptuous feast Kamikuu had left was gone. We filled the basket with sand wrapped in leaves and carried it to the cliff, where I tossed them into the sea. The food was in my body, the crime I had committed coursing through me. If I were to vomit now, would it be too late? The taste on my tongue reminded me of what I had done.

Mahito wrapped my trembling hand in his big palms. 'Namima. If we are to be punished, I will take your punishment, too.'

But I felt that a far greater calamity lay in store for me. Something Mahito could not ward off. I could not bring myself to answer.

When Mahito and I parted, I was terrified by the enormity of my crime. When Mother saw me, she stared at me expectantly, waiting for me to speak. But I said nothing.

The next morning I woke to find myself drenched with blood. At last my punishment had come – I was going to die. I began to scream. Mother ran in to me – and began to laugh. 'Namima, you've become a woman!'

And so I had – just like Kamikuu. I felt relieved. But when I remembered what I had done the night before, I imagined there must be a connection.

It was a clear, beautiful May morning, the day I became a woman. By noon I was restless and could not bear to be cooped up in the house. I went out by myself to the northern side of the island to collect the kuiko fruits that grew beside The Warning. Kamikuu and I had once crushed them with rocks and dyed our fingernails red with the juice. No one would celebrate my coming of age with me so I would have my own private celebration. My red fingernails reflected beautifully against the white sands and the bright blue sky. A gentle breeze wafted in from the seas, brushing lightly against my cheeks. The northern side of the island was the highest point and the breezes there were always cool and refreshing. My heart surged with optimism. Mahito. So long as I was with him, I'd endure any punishment.

When I got home, Mother caught sight of my red nails and asked what I'd been doing.

'I just peeled some kuiko,' I answered nonchalantly, trying to hide my hands. Mother averted her eyes. When Kamikuu had become a woman, Mother had steamed balls of rice dyed red with kuiko juice. Had my nails told her that I had seen those rice balls? I felt sure that Mahito's mother knew about our crime. I assumed that Kamikuu did, too. And now my mother? If so, it was only a matter of time before Mikura-sama and the island chief found out. The very idea was terrifying. But I could not forget my elation when I had stood at the northern cape feeling the breeze on my face.

Mahito and I continued secretly to eat the food Kamikuu left, indulging in what was forbidden, until Mahito's mother was again with child. We grew taller than those around us, our bodies plumper. Surely it was because we had secretly eaten the food Kamikuu had left that we were able to endure all that was to come our way – the arduous sea voyage and the birth of our Yayoi.

And so it was that my life took a dramatic turn. But I do not believe that the change was punishment for breaking the island law. I believe that it was because I broke the law that I was able to confront my true fate.

3

Four years passed. Then my life took the turn of which I have spoken. Mikura-sama died. Kamikuu was seventeen when it happened, and I was sixteen. While she was out on the Kyoido cape Mikura-sama collapsed and did not return home. It happened that the men were returning from their year-long fishing trip that day and saw her fall. She had been on the cape praying for their safe return. When the last vessel finally made port, she turned for home but cast a last look over her shoulder. That was when she fell. To me, it seemed prophetic. She fell in the exact spot where Mahito and I had met to exchange Kamikuu's leavings for bundles of sand. When I heard of Mikura-sama's death, of course I felt sad, but also relief; a sense of liberation. The more I thought about it, the more I came to understand how much I had feared Mikura-sama. And it was not only I: everyone on the island had been awed by her. Now she was gone. And I felt joyous.

My happiness was tinged, though, with guilt. My

relief was related to my sins. I wanted to talk to Mahito about my feelings, but the island was in uproar over Mikura-sama's death, and it was not safe for me to be seen in public with him. He still bore the taint of the curse. I knew the risks, but I needed to speak to him. I had something to tell him.

Mikura-sama had died so suddenly there had been no time to prepare for the grief. I wasn't even sure that what was happening was actually happening and I had to ask myself again and again whether or not I was dreaming. The uncertainty left me darkly apprehensive. One thing was clear, though: now that Mikura-sama was dead, Kamikuu's installation as the next Oracle was close. And so, even though the island was sunk in mourning Mikura-sama, there was a brightly buoyant undercurrent at the prospect of the young Kamikuu's future.

On our island children were considered adults once they turned sixteen. Boys were then allowed to set sail on the fishing vessels, and girls took part in the prayers and island rituals. When I became sixteen, I was called to join the women in the sacred precincts at the Kyoido and the Amiido. I had never imagined that my first prayer ritual would be occasioned by Mikura-sama's funeral.

Of course, my coming of age was marked by more than joining the other women in the prayers and rituals for the first time. I had a secret – a secret I could share with no one. Two months earlier, Mahito and I had begun to enjoy the ways of the flesh. The return of the fishing vessels, therefore, vexed us. Why? Because once the boats had returned, the night belonged to the young men. They would roam the island searching for available women. They ignored me because I had the important task of carrying Kamikuu's food to her in the evenings. Even so, I had to be particularly careful not to be caught with Mahito on the evenings when other young men were on the prowl.

Our island was governed by cruel customs. Food was rationed so only certain families were allowed to bear children, and this right had been decided in generations past. Any family associated with authority, such as those related to the island chief, might produce young. And so might families of long and noble lineage, or families such as mine and Mahito's, who were responsible for the island rituals. Because Mahito's family had failed to provide the island with an auxiliary *miko*, it had been cursed so Mahito and his brothers were forbidden to procreate.

Whatever the rules, though, men will lust after women, and babies will follow. The island chief required that all unlawful babies be put to death. Babies weren't the only ones. Whenever the chief noticed an increase in the number of old people, they would be rounded up and locked in a hut on the beach where they'd be left to starve to death. Such were the cruel customs on the island of my birth. I knew the rules, I knew the consequences, yet I could not contain my love for Mahito or my desire to be in his arms.

How sinful our love was! Our meetings always courted danger. We knew that we were treading a perilous precipice, that one step more would send us over the edge. But we could not stop. We were enchanted by the danger. Each time we reached the edge, we gladly stepped over, and each time, we loved each other more. And at that moment I felt, in the bottom of my heart, that I was far more fortunate than Kamikuu. I armed myself with this sense of superiority.

I was such a fool. Why? Because I carried Mahito's baby. And that was what I needed to discuss with him.

But let me return to Mikura-sama's funeral. For the first time in my life I wore the white ritual robes and stood in front of my house. The funeral procession, with Mikura-sama's coffin, went from the Kyoido, in the east of the island, to the western Amiido, where the dead were laid out. The men carrying the coffin were dressed in matching white garments. Their steps matched, too, as they walked slowly, solemnly, singing:

O Great Oracle,
Thou hast hidden;
O blessed sisters,
Both are hidden.

As the procession passed every house on the island, the members of the household joined it. By the time we reached the Amiido, it had grown very long. Of course, it had not crossed in front of Mahito's house since his family was cursed. The Umigame were banned even from the funeral.

I waited for the procession to near our house. My father and mother were there, with my brothers and uncles, all standing tensely. As the procession grew closer I noticed a second coffin, a small, simple one compared to Mikura-sama's elaborate box. Had Kamikuu died, too? My heart pounded at the thought. But no, Kamikuu was there, walking to the left of Mikura-sama's coffin, her posture upright and proud. I heaved a sigh of relief. I glanced at Kamikuu again, walking in the full sunlight. Her face was twisted with sorrow but it was so beautiful it glowed, perhaps because she was now to assume the duties of the Oracle in Mikura-sama's stead – but she also seemed tense.

When the island chief, who was leading the procession, reached my house, he murmured something to my father. My father turned to look at me and said, 'Namima. Walk beside the other coffin. Go with it to Amiido.'

I was about to ask him whose coffin it was when Mother motioned to me, as if to say, 'Hurry and do as you are told.' Confused, I rushed to join the procession. Kamikuu glanced at me and smiled faintly.

'Are you well?' I whispered.

She nodded.

'Whose coffin is this?' I asked.

'Nami-no-ue-sama,' Kamikuu replied. 'Woman-Upon-the-Waves.'

I'd never heard that name before. 'Who was she?'

'Mikura-sama's younger sister. She was our great-aunt.'

I hadn't known that Mikura-sama had a younger sister. I wanted to ask Kamikuu another question, but the burly men carrying the coffin came between us and I couldn't. The young men on our island were sturdily built, their skin burnt a coppery brown. They watched over Kamikuu and me with sharp eyes. But they could not conceal their fascination with Kamikuu's beauty. Kamikuu would have to marry one of the fishermen in due course, if she were to give birth to a daughter. If the union failed to produce a child, she would choose another man. The young men kept each other in check – competing to present a façade of propriety – while all the while they cast covert glances in Kamikuu's direction.

The procession finally reached the Amiido. A dark path opened like a slender tunnel between the thorny pandans and the banyan trees. It was so narrow we had to proceed in single file. It looked like the path that crossed beyond The Warning and led to the northern cape. I made my way through the tunnel behind Nami-no-ue-sama's coffin. Suddenly the thickets opened out on to a circular clearing. Straight ahead I could see the gaping entrance to a limestone cave. That must be where they took the island dead. Next to the cave there was a tiny thatched hut, perhaps for whoever tended the graves. The men placed Mikura-sama and Nami-no-ue-sama's coffins gently in front of the cave. I'd never seen the burial ground before and the sight of it now made me catch my breath. I wanted to leave as quickly as I could. It was a desolate, forbidding place.

Kamikuu drew to a stop and began to chant in a luminous voice:

Today, this very day
In the garden of the gods they hide;
In the garden of the gods they take pleasure;
In the garden of the gods they tarry;
From the heavens one descends,
From the seas one rises.
For today, this very day,
They pray.

The men answered Kamikuu's song, raising their voices raucously as they chanted the same words they had sung in the funeral procession. I followed what the other women were doing: they bent at the waist and clasped their hands together. The sturdy men stood and lifted the coffin, carrying it deep into the darkness of the cave. First Mikura-sama's coffin and next Nami-no-ue-sama's. Then, as though they were frightened of something, they cast their eyes to the ground and withdrew from the clearing. The women also kept their eyes trained on the ground and never glanced in the direction of the cave. They withdrew behind the men. So this was the Realm of the Dead. I had heard so much about it. The dead, we were told, travel along the underside of the island. I looked around curiously. Kamikuu came up beside me and began to chant the funeral procession song, her eyes on me.

O great Oracle,
Thou hast hidden;
O blessed sisters,
Both are hidden.

And then, as she blew upon a white shell, everyone turned back down the narrow path. I started to fall in behind the others. But the island chief and my father blocked my way.

'Namima – Woman-Amid-the-Waves – you are not to leave.'

I stood there petrified. What did they mean?

'From this day forth you will be the keeper of the Amiido. Kamikuu, Child of Gods, is *yang*. She is the high priestess who rules the realm of light. She resides at the Kyoido on the eastern edge of the island, where the sun rises. But you are *yin*. You must preside over the realm of darkness. You will live here, in the Amiido, on the western edge where the sun sets.'

I turned to stare in shock at the tiny hut standing just outside the cave that was filled with the bodies of the dead. So that was to be my house? I was in a daze.

The island chief barked an order: 'Namima! For the next twenty-nine days you will lift the lids of the coffins and check that Mikura-sama and Nami-no-ue-sama have not come back to life. You will never be allowed to return to the village. Food will be left for you at the entrance to the Amiido. You will eat this food. There is a small well behind the hut. You will not lack for anything.'

'I may not live with my mother and father again – ever?'

When I asked this, my father, who was burnt black by the sun, said sadly, 'We will meet again when we die.'

'I can't do this! Father, please, help me! Mother!'

I clung to the hem of my father's white garment. But he prised my hands away.

'Namima, you must control yourself. We could not tell you because it had to come from Kamikuu. You were born into the most important family on the island and destined to become the high priestess of the darkness. It is your fate and you are powerless to change it. You are here to guide the dead so that they will find their way safely to the world of darkness. You must acquit yourself with pride.'

I understood now why Kamikuu had looked at me earlier with eyes so full of pity.

'But Kamikuu said none of this to me!'

The island chief and my father looked at each other

in surprise. The chief spoke to me sternly: 'I will remind you of the island law. The eldest daughter, born of the Oracle's household, serves the realm of light. The second daughter serves the realm of darkness. After the sun has warmed the island during the day, it sinks beneath the island into the seas where it shines along the seabed and there makes its way back to the surface and rises again in the east. The eldest daughter protects the daylight, the younger the night; it is her duty to govern the bottom of the sea. On our island the night becomes the world of the dead. The elder daughter is responsible for continuing the Oracle's lineage. She must give birth to a daughter. The second sister's lineage ends at one generation. She must not have union with a man.'

The island chief gazed into the western sky as he spoke. The sun was just beginning to slip into the sea dyeing his white beard red.

'Wait, sir!' I begged. 'If Nami-no-ue-sama were charged with protecting the island at night, why did I never know about her? And why is she being buried at the same time as Mikura-sama?'

The island chief let out a deep sigh. 'When Mikura-sama became the Oracle, Nami-no-ue-sama entered that hut. She lived here henceforth all alone. So, no one ever saw her. Of course, the adults would enter the Amiido whenever there was a funeral, and they would see Nami-no-ue-sama then.'

'But how is it that she died at the same time that Mikura-sama died?'

'When the sun does not rise again, the night, too, must not return.'

What did he mean? That when Mikura-sama died, Nami-no-ue-sama could not continue living? Was that why we had prayed so fervently for Mikura-sama's long life? By the same token, I would now have to pray that Kamikuu lived long, too, wouldn't I? Is that what Mother had meant when she told me that Kamikuu and I were born to be opposites? I hadn't understood it when she had told me that Kamikuu was *yang* and I was *yin*, or when Mikura-sama had said I was 'impure'. *I was the impure one.* But Mahito and I had eaten food that had been prepared for Kamikuu. We had been united in love. And now I was carrying his child. When I thought about all my transgressions, I was so terrified I fainted.

When I came to my senses, the sun had set and I was surrounded by darkness. I had been lying in the soft grass at the centre of the circle. Of course, no one was there now. The moon was out, and I could see the coffins that had been placed inside the cave. When I looked closer I could see what appeared to be other coffins further back.

Lots of them. I had never seen a dead body, and I was so frightened that I began to crawl across the ground on my hands and knees, clutching the long grass. I began to think I might as well be dead myself. I'd be better off. I thought of throwing myself into the sea. I'd have to leave the Amiido to do so. It would take all my strength to scale the surrounding cliff.

I began to search for the pathway out, peering hard in the moonlight. Eventually I found the tunnel in the thicket of trees. But as I tried to push my way through it, I discovered that a gate had been placed across the path, making it impossible for me to leave. I was locked inside the burial grounds. My father and brothers were standing in the darkness on the other side of the gate. Overjoyed, I rushed towards them, calling, 'Father! Elder Brother! Please – help me open the gate.'

'The gate will remain where it is for the twenty-nine-day watch. We'll take it down after that. It is here so that we can be sure that the spirits of the newly dead do not leave the Amiido and wander the island.'

The older of my brothers spoke in a hushed tone. Normally they were not particularly kind to me, probably because their father and the father I shared with Kamikuu were not the same. But tonight I heard gentleness in his voice.

'Brother, I'm afraid to stay here all by myself. How can I live here for twenty-nine days?'

Uncertain what to say, he cast his eyes to the ground. I thrust my arms through the gate and grabbed my father, but he pushed my hands away.

'Namima, I am sorry for you, but there is nothing I can do. No one can challenge the island's laws. Kamikuu must live alone and devote her life to the prayers and rituals. You must live with the dead. We men must set out to fish and spend our days plying the seas. Others must go hungry. On this island, we live the lives allotted to us, or we become like the Umigame family, left by the wayside to rot.'

My father spoke in such a low voice that the ends of his sentences were swallowed by the sound of the waves. I found it difficult to hear him. But I understood one thing with perfect clarity. I could not escape. I was to spend my life locked up here with the dead, like Nami-no-ue-sama before me, tending whatever new corpse was delivered to me. And if, before Kamikuu herself died, I was delivered of a child, it would surely be killed by the island chief once people found out. Before I knew it, I was screaming, 'I want to see my mother! Please bring her here.'

My brother was disgusted by my outburst. 'You are

no longer a child, Namima! Didn't Kamikuu leave the family when she was just six to start her training to become the Oracle? You lived at home and enjoyed a happy childhood. That's enough!'

I continued to weep and wail, but my father and brothers set off down the path, refusing to turn back. I stood beside the gate until the break of day. I was terrified of the burial ground. Those nights when I had taken the dark path home from Mikura-sama's cottage seemed a dream – the nights when I had encountered Mahito, secretly shared with him the sacred food and lain with him. Now I had been thrown into this unfamiliar world, held there by a formidable gate. I could see The Warning in the distance, past which I could never set foot again. And when I thought that I would never be able to see Mahito, I was so choked with sorrow I could hardly breathe.

When day finally broke, I pushed my fears aside and turned back to the burial grounds. I went inside Nami-no-ue-sama's tiny hut. It was rustic, cramped and worn. The sunlight filtering in revealed a tilting shelf and neatly arranged on it were a spoon and a pair of chopsticks made of turban shell, a small bowl fashioned from a coconut that had most likely washed ashore, and a few other utensils. I had never met Nami-no-ue-sama, but when I saw the frugality of her life, I found myself giving way again to uncontrollable sobs. I would be next to live this life.

Suddenly I wanted to know who Nami-no-ue-sama had been. I wanted to see her face. I turned with determination and walked into the cave. The deeper part was packed with coffins in all stages of decay. There were tiny ones among the rest that I imagined belonged to Mahito's baby brothers. The damp, mouldy smell of decomposition that wafted to me was horrible beyond description. The two new coffins were at the mouth of the cave. I lifted the lid slowly from the smaller, rough-hewn one and saw the body of an old woman, slight of build and with long white hair. I gasped. This was the woman I had seen on the first night I had delivered Kamikuu's food. The person I had thought was a goddess. She looked like Mikura-sama. By the time I was born she was already in the Amiido, serving as the priestess of the darkness.

'You lived at home and enjoyed a happy childhood!' I remembered my brother's words to me last night. Kamikuu had purposely chosen not to tell me of this. She knew that Mahito and I had been eating her leavings. It was thanks to her that I had been able to enjoy a happy childhood. But had I really? I could still feel the pressure of Mikura-sama's finger, so long ago on Kamikuu's birthday.

That gesture had foretold the end of my 'happy child-hood'. People might not have gossiped about me outright, but I felt they had looked upon me as someone to be pitied or despised because I had been pronounced impure.

No one had told me about Nami-no-ue-sama because they saw me as they had seen her – as someone beneath notice. It was as if we were invisible. They had not behaved out of spite – yet somehow it was malicious. To them, I was no better than a tiny black grain of sand at the bottom of the sea. Deep on the ocean floor, where the rays of the sun never reach. How appropriate that the priestess of the darkness was given governance of the bottom of the sea.

What about Mahito? My heart froze. No one would deliver food to Kamikuu now, would they? Surely she would be besieged with marriage proposals from the island youth, eager to assist her in producing the next generation of Oracle and priestess of the darkness.

Mikura-sama's reign was over. That truth took hold of me as I glanced at the other new coffin in the cave. I was the only one there in the dark, the only one locked up with the dead. And if I had never met Mahito, I would not have been so troubled by it.

★

Another night approached. I had opened the two coffins and looked at the faces of the dead. But once it grew dark I was terrified to be in there alone. I thought about Nami-no-ue-sama spending her life there by herself and my eyes welled with tears. But on the night I had seen her she had slipped out of the Amiido and gone to wander the shores of the dark sea.

The realm of night is the realm of the dead. It is a realm beyond the reach of the sun's rays. A realm deep beneath the waves on the ocean's floor. While the sun slowly circled the island, I must wander among the boulders on the ocean floor where there was no light, offering prayers for the dead. I didn't know how to go about this. I sat trembling inside the hut, waiting for the sun to return.

I heard footsteps. The spirits and ghosts must have slipped from the cave to surround the hut. They had come for me, the newcomer. I had no idea how to calm a restless spirit. I remembered what the other women had done when the funeral procession had reached the graveyard: I clasped my hands together and bowed with all my might. My teeth were chattering with fear. There was a knock.

'Namima, open the door.'

Mahito? I was too stunned to move. The door opened,

and in the moonlight I saw the tall figure of a man step across the threshold. Mahito had come for me, even to this defiled place. Overjoyed, I leapt into his arms. His chest was warm and his heart was beating wildly. As we embraced each other, I understood what it meant to be alive. I loved Mahito and I could not pull myself from his arms.

'Mahito, I—'

He put his finger over my lips to stop my words. 'I know. But Mikura-sama may hear us. We must be quiet.'

I shuddered to think that we had to be wary even of the dead. But her spirit was probably still wandering this world. We had to be cautious. I whispered to Mahito, as tears trickled down my cheeks, 'I'm carrying your baby.'

Surprise suffused his face. He thought for a minute and then murmured, his voice strong, 'Namima, we have to leave the island.'

Even if we had a boat, the waves were fierce – and the island men had their fishing vessels moored on the offing not far away: if we tried to sail to a neighbouring island, they would catch us and bring us back. I had heard that far away there was a large island known as Yamato. No one had ever sailed that far.

'I'll get a boat and some provisions. I want you to wait for me.'

I nodded, as if I were in a dream. I wondered if Mikura-sama's ghost could hear us. 'Mahito, please wait until the twenty-nine days are over.'

'That's too long.'

I, too, doubted I could wait until then. But I felt such pity for Nami-no-ue-sama, forgotten by her family and forced to stay in a place where she had contact with others only at a funeral. Nami-no-ue-sama had smiled at me on that night long ago. I wanted to see off her spirit to the next world.

'I'll come back for you.'

As soon as Mahito had said this, he disappeared into the darkness. I was certain my father and brothers were keeping watch at the entrance to the Amiido, making sure I didn't try to escape. Mahito must have slipped in by a different way. I prayed that no one would see him depart. And I prayed for the repose of Mikura-sama and Nami-no-ue-sama's spirits. I placed my trust in Mahito.

After a few days had passed, the skin on Mikura-sama and Nami-no-ue-sama's faces began to split. Decomposition set in. The smell of death wafted through the cave anew. I was frightened, but I kept watch over the decaying bodies of the two women. They were just like the decayed bodies of animals, I told myself. I had to remain strong.

One night Mahito came to me. He entered the hut quietly and took me in his arms. I sensed his excitement, and felt myself return to life. He spoke quickly, in hushed tones: 'Namima, I've heard that your mother is so worried about you she comes every day to the entrance of the Amiido. Kamikuu is intended to marry Ichi, the first son of the Samé family – namesakes of the Shark. The nuptials will be held when the twenty-nine days are over. If you and I are to escape, we should do it on the night of their wedding. Everyone will be drunk and distracted and the men will postpone their fishing until it's over.'

I let out a sigh of relief. Lately my belly had begun to swell. So long as I was in the Amiido, no one would know that I was with child, but when it was discovered that the one burdened with the defilement of death was not a virgin, the island chief would probably have me killed.

'You have a boat?'

'My younger brothers helped me. They repaired my grandfather's old one. And we've stocked up on food.'

I brushed my cheek against Mahito's arm. 'Mahito, how do you know your way into the Amiido?'

'I came to tend my dead baby brothers. I knew Nami-no-ue-sama.'

I wondered if she had known what Mahito and I would

do. I wanted to ask Mahito if he had told her, but he slipped quietly from the hut. 'I'll come again,' he said, before he left.

Mahito came every other night. His visits kept me alive. Every day I ate the food that someone had placed in front of the gate for me – just as I had done for Kamikuu. I drank the water from the well behind the hut. And every morning I lifted the lids of the two coffins and checked the bodies inside. Gradually the flesh was melting away. Whenever heavy rain fell, the damp seeped even to the back of the cave, and the smell of decay was overpowering.

One night I thought I heard footsteps circling the hut. I started to call Mahito's name but caught myself at the last minute and clamped my mouth shut. There was more than one pair of feet. Had a group come from the village? I was scared, but I opened the door and peered out. Mikura-sama and Nami-no-ue-sama were standing together in the clearing. They had been restored to their former selves and were fondly holding each other's hands.

'Thank you, Namima,' Mikura-sama greeted me. 'We shall leave now.'

Nami-no-ue-sama smiled sweetly and waved a delicate hand. They seemed to glide over the grass until they disappeared into the thicket. The moon shone brightly as I followed them quietly. My fear had left me. They had looked happy and I felt compelled to pursue them. They began to climb the cliff behind the Amiido with some effort. Once they reached the top, they stepped off into the sea, where once again they seemed to glide along the surface. As I watched them go, I realised that my twenty-nine-day vigil had ended. I sat on the ground and wept.

The next morning when I walked to the Amiido entrance the gate had gone. I was the priestess of the darkness. I knew that, gate or no gate, I was not to walk to the village under the light of day. I was the priestess of the dead, a defiled person.

That night I heard the wedding festivities from my hut in the Amiido. They were sounding the large taikô drum and plucking the two-stringed bow. The voices of the merrymakers reverberated throughout the island. Mahito came to me. I clung to his hand, and when I left Nami-no-ue-sama's hut, I carried with me the spoon made of shell and nothing more. We walked together through the darkness.

We passed The Warning and went down the road to the northern cape. We took care not to get caught on the pandan thorns and worked our way slowly northward. Mahito's boat was moored at the northern cape, where only the Oracles had ever set foot. The waves there were large and might swallow our little vessel or cast us upon an unknown island. But we pressed ahead, holding one another's hand. I was not afraid. I was going to an unfamiliar land, and there I would give birth to Mahito's babies, one after another. Freedom! My heart bounced in my chest just like a ball. I gazed at Mahito's profile. He carried a pine-branch torch as we pressed on through the pandan thicket. I loved him with all my heart. I would gladly have given my life for him.

INTO THE REALM OF THE DEAD

1

My death came with no warning. There was no wind that night, no waves, and the moon and stars had not yet appeared. The night was so dark and still it was as if everything and everyone in the world had come to a standstill. That was when it happened.

The little boat that held my husband, Mahito, our little baby and me rocked gently, softly, like a cradle. In the pure darkness, the waves were barely perceptible. I held my baby to my breast, and Mahito, sitting behind me, wrapped me in his arms. We slept peacefully.

Suddenly I awoke to a horrible unease. I opened my eyes and looked around me but saw nothing. The sky was black and endless. It was as if time had ceased. The magnitude of the firmament pressed down upon me, like a dark canopy.

I had grown weak. The long sea voyage had worn me down. But I was also exhausted by childbirth. Just days before I had given birth to a daughter aboard the tiny boat. And what a painful birth it had been. I had screamed through the agony for a full day and night. Then, when it was over, and I held my precious tiny daughter to my breast, I was intoxicated by a supreme joy: I had fulfilled a most important duty and we would soon be at Yamato. If I felt any uncertainty, it was brought on by worry for the wellbeing of my child, born at sea. Would she reach land safely? It never once occurred to me that I would be the one to die. I gave my daughter the name Yayoi, for it meant 'the deep of night'.

Up to that point our journey had been so smooth it was little short of miraculous. Occasionally we chanced upon a storm severe enough to sink our little boat in the blink of an eye, yet we managed to sail around it. We were at sea for more than half a year, and any number of misfortunes might have befallen us, but we met none. Mahito and I remained healthy. It was as if we had been blessed with great good fortune, as if someone were watching over us. Of course, that did not mean we never despaired of reaching our destination, but those moments were rare and chased away by another stroke of luck.

There would be days, for example, when our drinking water was on the brink of running dry, and a big black cloud would bubble up on the horizon to deliver sweet, warm rain. When our food gave out, we would find ourselves surrounded by a school of tiny fish. Seafaring birds, worn out by their long journeys, would drop down into our boat — as if to say, please, eat me! Just when we were at the point of exhaustion and able to go no further, a gentle breeze would guide our little boat to a sandbar where we could rest. Drifting imperceptibly in the midst of the great sea, they were made of coral and were delicate little formations of land. Too tiny to be called islands — and easily obscured by a large wave crashing over them — they were like floating mirages. And strangest of all, at the heart of those pretty little sandbars there would be a bubbling fountain of fresh water ringed by fan palms. How was it possible to find land such as this in the middle of the sea? Even as we half doubted, half believed what we beheld, when our feet sank into the sand after so many months at sea we would be overcome with joy. We would fill our mouths with green leaves, and drink the cool water until our bellies ached. And then, when we turned back to our boat and the long, long journey that still lay ahead of us, we would feel refreshed, our spirits restored.

Perhaps all of this good fortune befell us just so that I might safely deliver my precious daughter. And by the same token perhaps it was also pre-ordained that I would die just before reaching Yamato. That was as it had to be: I was to go to the goddess to serve at her side. But at the time I knew none of this and, drunk with happiness, I believed that – Mahito and I, so young and strong, could do anything. Such arrogance!

On the day my daughter was born, perhaps because the weather was surprisingly clear, we could see the looming shape of an island on the horizon ahead of us. My heart quickened in anticipation.

'That must be Yamato. Our long, difficult journey is coming to an end,' Mahito whispered, as I lay on my side, eyes closed. I was exhausted, but managed to smile, spurred by hope. When we reached Yamato, Mahito told me, we would build a little cottage by the sea where we would live, poor but happy. That was what he told me, over and over again. How delighted I was, knowing that my daughter had escaped the fate that would have been hers on our island.

And how wrong I had been! It had always been my destiny to become the priestess of the darkness, my lot from birth – no, even before birth. But I had sought to defy fate. I had fallen in love with a man who was cursed, fled the island with him and borne his child. Even though my sins were many, the goddess did not punish me. Rather she drew me to her. How grateful I was for her leniency.

2

Awakened by unease, I found myself staring up into the night sky. In the distance I heard fish leaping from the sea. I turned to look and caught the shimmer of lightning far away, illuminating the jet black sky. In that one brief second, I glimpsed the white crests of the waves stretching as far as the eye could see. I knew we were still at sea but I felt as if we were wandering over a vast, dark wilderness. Seized with fear, I clung to my daughter, terrified she would be wrested away from me.

'What is it?' Mahito asked, startled by my movements.

'I'm frightened.'

As I spoke I felt my chest constrict. I could not breathe. I tried to scream but I could make no sound.

And then I realised that the pressure on my throat was made by Mahito's warm fingers. He was behind me, strangling me. Mahito? Why was he trying to kill me? I couldn't believe it. Yet the fingers on my throat were his. I tore violently at them. Little Yayoi at my breast began to shriek.

And then, just before I drew my last breath, I heard Mahito say, in an agonised voice, 'Namima, forgive me.'

I died alone, confused. I'd had no hint of what was to befall me. Those parting words had come so suddenly; – 'Namima, forgive me.' Gradually my body grew cold, but I could still hear his trembling voice, feel the tears streaking down my cheeks, and Yayoi's tiny lips on my breast. My senses lived on, but my body grew stiff, and as the days wore past my stomach began to rot. My senses faded.

Mahito prepared my corpse for disposal. He dressed my hair with white ornaments he had fashioned out of fish bones and adorned my body with the feathers of sea birds and the sea grass he had collected as they drifted by. When he had finished, he cast my body into the sea.

I lay on the dark sea floor, my bones slowly sinking into the sands. For a time, I remained vaguely aware, my senses diminished but still present. Gradually, though, they, too, disappeared. Only my consciousness remained. Tiny fish feasted on the flesh that clung to my skeleton. And when it had been consumed, I was nothing but bones.

I had felt such joy in turning my back on the island taboo, taking charge of my own destiny – until my sudden death. Why had Mahito done this to me? Mahito, my beloved. Distraught, confused, I moaned in anguish. But there was nothing I could do now. I lay alone at the bottom of the dark sea. The sands of the ocean floor cradled me, and each wave that passed rocked my bones back and forth. It was as though the swells were caused by the tears my sister Kamikuu and my mother Nisera must be shedding for me. 'Poor, poor Namima.' I could imagine their lament. In time, I grew calmer. Both Mikura-sama and Nami-no-ue-sama still walked the seas and I could feel their tender gaze on my back. It was strange, of course, for I had no back, no visible shape, yet I could sense warmth creep softly up my spine, and I began to feel happy again. Before long I became used to my life on the ocean floor.

When my senses returned to me again, I was in a darkness so complete I could not see my fingers in front of my face, but I could tell that I was no longer at sea. I was lying face up on damp ground. I opened my eyes and looked around, searching for a sign of life. No one was near by. I no longer felt the presence of Kamikuu or my mother. When I realised that I was completely alone I grew so distraught that my sorrow was nearly unbearable. But wait – wasn't I dead? How could I feel anything at all? My corpse had sunk to the ocean floor and dissolved into tiny pieces, like decayed coral. I knew I was now no more than grains of sand.

Slowly I felt for my breasts, which, not very long ago, had been so full that they gushed milk, wetting Yayoi's lips. But my body was now empty – there was nothing to touch, nothing to touch with. Time passed. I stood and tried to walk – I took one step, and then another, gingerly, unsteadily. I seemed to be in a tunnel. Far, far ahead I could make out a sliver of a light. I headed towards it along a dark, narrow path.

I came to what looked like an opening. But a huge boulder had been wedged into it, as if to block the way. Thin ribbons of light streamed in along the edges. I gazed at my fingers. The light shone right through them.

'Namima, how good of you to come.'

I heard a low, raspy voice behind me. When I turned towards it, I saw a woman standing on the path below me dressed in white, her long hair piled high atop her head. She was walking towards me. She seemed of noble birth and light emanated from her body. She looked slightly younger than my mother, but she was so very thin and haggard that she might have been older even than Mikura-sama. Her brows were knitted in irritation.

'Namima, don't be alarmed. Please, come closer.'

I walked towards her. When I drew near, I stopped and bowed, trembling. 'I am Namima, Woman-Amid-the-Waves, of Umihebi, the Island of Sea Snakes.'

'I know well who you are, Namima. You are the priestess of the darkness, are you not? Before you arrived I had no one to keep me company so I am delighted to see you.'

'I am grateful for your kindness, but may I ask your name?'

'Izanami, Goddess of the Underworld.'

Her voice was expressionless, and for a goddess she seemed miserable.

I had never heard the name Izanami before. But she was clearly not a human being and I was too terrified to raise my head to look at her. She said she was a goddess – a god – so she must be. But she did not look at all as I had imagined a goddess would. When I lived on the island the goddess I had dreamt of had had a kind and gentle face.

'Namima, look at me.'

Slowly, I looked up. Izanami was standing right beside me. I nearly shrieked with fear. Her face was perplexing. Her eyebrows were drawn tightly together in a deep frown. At one moment she seemed ready to rage and at the next as though she might cry. I had never met anyone with such an unreadable face.

In a low voice, Izanami said, 'This is Yomi, the Realm of the Dead. Now that you are here, you may never return to the world of the living.'

'The Realm of the Dead?'

'Yes.'

I could never return to the world of the living. Then it was true. Mahito had killed me. Suddenly I felt again his fingers on my throat and a shiver crept up my spine. I realised I was crying. I could feel tears coursing down my cheeks. When I had been locked into the Amiido burial grounds, I'd been scared out of my wits. But though Amiido had been a realm of death, it had still coursed with life. This place, on the other hand, showed not the slightest hint of it. It was truly the world of the dead.

'You're crying, aren't you, Namima? This must seem a very lonely place.'

Izanami had spoken gently. I brought my transparent fingers to my cheeks. How strange that I could tell they were damp with icy tears.

'Namima, instead of crying, look about you. We are standing on an incline that is known as Yomotsuhira-saka – the Yomi Slope. Just ahead, at the top of the slope, is the pass between the Realm of the Dead and the world of the living.'

Izanami's voice was filled with sorrow. I raised my eyes. She spread her slender hand above my head, as if to shelter my eyes from the light that leaked through my fingers.

'My husband, Izanaki, put that boulder there to block the passage, so I am trapped here for all eternity.'

Izanami's speech grew harsh, betraying a touch of despair. The angrier she became, the more brilliant the light that emanated from her. I turned my head to avoid it and asked, 'Before he did that, were you able to go back and forth between worlds?' I would be lying if I said there wasn't the faintest suggestion of hope in my question. I might have been dead and no longer in possession of my earthly body, but I couldn't help wanting to go back to the world of the living. I wanted to know what had become of Mahito and Yayoi. If only I could find out why he had done what he'd done . . . if only I could see the kind of woman Yayoi would become . . .

'If someone from the other world should want to enter this one, they may do so.'

Izanami stood with her back to the boulder, the sliver of light behind her. Although her body was as emaciated as a withered branch, she still had a regal bearing. She lifted her arm high and pointed to the dark tunnel that spread out beneath her.

'Namima. This path leads to the Palace of the Dead. It is as cold as ice there, dark and completely empty. Izanaki and I were once a happy couple yet here I am alone, separated from him for ever by death.'

I looked down at the dark tunnel leading deep into the earth. It was as if I were entering a tomb. Was I to serve this goddess and spend the rest of eternity in this underworld? I was assailed by fresh despair.

On the island where I was born, the dead were laid out in the burial grounds long enough for their spirits to be pacified. Eventually they would depart, alone, for the bottom of the sea. We believed the underside of the island was the world of the dead. We had come to this belief by watching the passage of the sun. After the sun has warmed the island during the day, it sinks into the seas beneath the island, where it shines along the seabed and then makes its way back to the surface to rise again in the east. Whenever we dived into the sea and saw the beauty below, we believed it was there for the dead, which made us feel calm and happy. The rays of the sun might not reach to the deepest ocean floors, but lovely sea grasses grew on the whitest of sands. Cool waters streamed through like breezes and gently caressed the bones of the dead. But in this dark underworld, there were no fish to nibble the bones, no soft sea grasses to twine about the feet. There was nothing but dark, fetid air and the smell of earth.

'Izanami, are the dead not allowed ever to leave?'

'Until someone moves the boulder, we are here for ever in this cold, dark tomb.'

Izanami was ahead of me. She did not look back as she spoke.

The boulder. Proof that our worlds connected. The boulder reminded me of The Warning on my island, the abrupt landmark on the road that passed to the northern cape. No one was allowed to set foot beyond that rock. But I had, hadn't I? I had travelled beyond The Warning and had ended up here in the Realm of the Dead. The memory filled me with sorrow.

'But that is not to say there is no other way out.' Suddenly Izanami turned to face me. She stared directly into my eyes, as if trying to discover some hidden truth there. 'Do you want to go back, Namima? You can't return in your living form. But if you want to return, I will tell you how you may.'

I was too confused to speak. Izanami pulled her shoulders back and, with a knowing air, said, 'But you shouldn't, you know. As soon as you return you'll feel such envy for the living. You'll wonder why it was you who came to such a pass. It will only bring you sadness. Namima, the Realm of the Dead is the place that welcomes those spirits who have nowhere else to go. Restless souls come here – those who burn with hatred, who still feel love, those unable to float free of their earthly longings.'

She was right. I hated Mahito and still felt such profound love for Yayoi. I longed to know how she was. The Realm of the Dead was the perfect place for a woman like me.

3

The pitch darkness was all around me, but when I listened carefully I could hear from time to time – just barely – the sound of waves and, way off in the distance, a faint beating 'zaza . . . zaza . . .' as if the earth itself were pulsating. Having grown up on an island, I felt a keen unease every time I heard something like that, imagining that the sound signalled to the spirits of the dead that they should awaken. The island of my birth, with its beautiful white coral-sand beaches that glittered in the sun, was tiny, easily swallowed by the seas when a storm brewed. But one thing was constant: the sound of the waves. Beneath the earth in the sunless darkness, my heart was torn asunder to hear what must have been the waves. The sound reminded me all the more of the hopelessness of my fate. At the same time, it urged me to question Izanami. She was lost in thought, her beautiful brows knitted, her eyes downcast, as if she were troubled. I bided my time and, when the opportunity arose, I asked.

'Izanami-sama, that sound . . . in the distance . . . Is it waves? Are we near the sea?'

Izanami stared off into the distance, as if she were pondering her response. But she was not looking at anything in particular. Only darkness lay before her. Our underground palace was illuminated by the faint glow of will-o'-the-wisps. The cold, meagre light they provided seemed to trap us in their orbit. Beyond this, I came to realise, there was limitless darkness. I would never escape it. I understood that. Yet as the spark at the inner core of my being grew colder, I found myself assailed by glimmers of hope. I was brooding over this when Izanami finally spoke, her voice grave.

'Yomotsuhira-saka, which separates the living from the dead, is located where the earth and the sea part. What you've heard, Namima, are the echoes of the waves, I suppose.'

The place where I had been lying earlier, then, would have been the entrance to a cave facing the sea. It was profoundly moving to think that the waves I was hearing now existed in the world of the living. It made me wish all the more to return to the earlier nothingness of death. Why had I been brought here? Why must I suffer again the desires and heartache I had known when I was alive?

'Izanami-sama, what has brought me here? I was dead,

wasn't I? I want to return to that oblivion. When I died, I was separated from the living for all eternity. I want to sleep at peace, free of everything. Please, let me return to death.'

'Namima, neither you nor I are allowed that nothingness. You are well suited to this existence. You are the priestess of the darkness so who better than you?'

I looked at the palace hall around me. Huge stone pillars towered above the cold rock floor, each set at an equal distance from the next. There were so many pillars that I could not count them. They extended as far as the eye could see, the distant ones melting into the darkness. They were massive, so wide that three people could join hands around one and still not encircle the girth, and so tall that the tops disappeared into the darkness above. The Yomi Palace seemed to go on for ever into an infinite space.

In the shadows cast by the pillars servants stood at hushed attention ready to answer Izanami's call. Here and there I caught glimpses of spirits, hovering in human form.

'Those who cannot free themselves of their attachments come to the Realm of the Dead. Most are spirits who prowl through the darkness. They have no form, no feelings, no thoughts. They are merely the lingering spirits of former human beings. Look around you,

Namima. It may look like darkness to you, but countless spirits are all around us.'

'I've begun to sense their presence.'

As I spoke a host of nameless spirits closed in around me and I could feel the dark air grow dense with their presence: the spirits of humans who had died with unresolved desires. Suddenly overcome by an unease I could not name, I drew back and spoke once again to Izanami: 'Is Nami-no-ue-sama here?'

'She is not. She fulfilled her destiny.'

I remember how she had smiled at me. Nami-no-ue-sama, Woman-Upon-the-Waves. She had ended her life with Mikura-sama's and had acquitted herself well. But apparently I was not to share a similar ending.

'And Mikura-sama? Is she here?'

'Mikura is not here either.'

'Where are they?'

Izanami pointed above her. 'They are in the heavens with the gods, I suppose.'

Confused, I peered into her face. 'But, Izanami-sama, aren't you a god as well? Why aren't you in the heavens? Why are you here?'

Izanami answered coldly, 'I was sent here as the goddess who governs the Realm of the Dead, the deity of the underworld.'

'But how did that come about?'

'Because my husband, Izanaki, came late to visit me. And then he broke his promise. I bear a grudge against my husband, Namima, just as you do.'

Izanami's explanation left me even more baffled than before. I did not know the particulars of the quarrel between Izanami and Izanaki; and I was just as uncertain of the qualities I had that had brought me to serve her. She had said it was because I was the priestess of the darkness. But I had fled my post and broken the law of the island.

'Izanami-sama, earlier you said that I was suited to this place because I was the priestess of the darkness. But I gave birth to a child and that alone disqualified me from my role.'

Izanami's lips curled slightly upward in what appeared to be a smile. 'It is precisely because you bore a child that you are perfectly suited to serve me. For me, there is a deep connection between death and birth. I died in childbirth, you see.'

'Really? And my husband killed me after I had delivered.'

'I pity you, Namima. My death was not nearly as bitter as yours. After I died, my husband came to the Realm of the Dead to meet me, and we were separated after that.'

It surprised me that Izanami, who had clearly died long, long ago, was able to feel sympathy for me. That must be because my fate had been so much more tragic than anyone else's. But what *had* happened to me? Why had I met such an end? I could feel the darkness of angry uncertainty creeping over me. Was there any way to escape it?

4

A single day in the underground Realm of the Dead passed slowly, much more so than days in the world of the living. While I was serving Izanami, Mahito must have grown old and Yayoi had matured into a woman. Or perhaps she was already old. Were they still living? If they had died, they would have died peacefully, that much I knew. Otherwise they would have been here.

Izanami knew all about the unquiet dead. Every day she selected a thousand people to die. This was her main task. We were sure to hear from those who were unable to go quietly, whose restless spirits lingered to complain. Today a host of men and women were lined up outside Izanami's chambers clamouring to get in, a dazed, unfocused look on their faces.

Izanami, attired in white robes, spent almost all her time in her dimly lit chamber. A map of the living world was spread at the centre of the room. When I had first glanced at it, it had resembled an enormous dry lake bed. But staring intently into the darkness, I soon saw it featured oceans and islands. Tall mountains soared upward and rivers cut deep channels. Izanami stood before the diagram of Yamato and paced backwards and forwards. She held a transparent white bowl filled with black water, which she sprinkled on the map below. The water was drawn, every morning, by her servants from a well within the palace.

If Izanami's water drops landed on a person, they would die – unless they were already to die because of illness, an accident or old age. Among those, it was only the restless who made their way to the Realm of the Dead – those unable to float free of their desires. When Izanami decided on her deaths, I stood beside her to render service. I wondered, as I stood there, how it was that such a beautiful goddess had come to perform such an unpleasant task.

One day, the droplets of black water flew to the top of a mountain peak and splashed my cheek. The chill made me shudder and I raised my hand to wipe it away.

'Izanami-sama, do you know before you begin who you will mark with the water of death?'

Izanami turned towards me. 'I select them.'

'How?'

'I kill all the women with whom Izanaki has been united.'

I caught my breath. 'How do you know who they are?'

'He has assumed the guise of a human man and travels far and wide. But I receive reports from all kinds of living things, and from the dead as well. I am able to follow him wherever he goes. He will never be able to escape my hand of death.'

'But you don't kill Izanaki.'

Izanami turned to me with a blank look. 'Izanaki is a god. He cannot die.'

'But you did.'

Izanami's face clouded. 'I am a god, that's true. But I died because of childbirth. It's always the woman who dies.' A deep bitterness seeped into her eyes, along with a look of resignation. What was going through her mind? What had happened to her? My heart begins to tremble. What power had I to protect myself now? Of course, I was already dead. It wasn't as though she or anyone else could kill me again. What did I have to be afraid of? And yet I was terrified.

'Izanami-sama, I would be very grateful if you would tell me how it was you became the Goddess of the Underworld. I would like to know of your pain, your sufferings.' I made a concerted effort to look directly at her as I spoke.

Izanami opened her eyes wide but – perhaps because

she had spent so much time surrounded by darkness –
they had no focus. I thought she was looking at me but
I couldn't be sure. I stared intently at her eyes, finding
it difficult to distinguish the darkness of the palace from
their own. A few more minutes passed and then Izanami
finally began to speak.

'At last I have someone who will listen to what I have
to say. I can unburden my heart and give vent to all my
feelings. I live here trapped – tied to this wheel of
suffering. Since I found myself locked in the Realm of
the Dead, I have spent my time selecting those who are
to die. It brings me some relief. But then, when I think
about him, such hatred wells up within me – it is all the
more intense because it has nowhere to go. So I suffer.
Of course, deciding who will die is not something that
should give joy. It pains those who are selected, and I
must shoulder the burden of their suffering for all eternity. Namima, do you know what the worst feeling in
the world is? Hatred. Now I must wait for the fires of
my hatred to be extinguished. Until that happens, there
can be no peace. But when will the fires die out? It was
thanks to Izanaki that I was forced into this cold, dark
tomb beneath the earth, and as long as I am trapped here,
the fires of hatred will never die. Please, hear me out.'

5

Izanami's tone took on a heightened formality.

'I shall speak of the creation of our world, thousands and thousands of years before you were born, Namima. Far, far in the ancient past, there was nothing, no earth, no land, just roiling chaos. From this disorder the teeming matter was divided into heaven and earth. And following this came further divisions, each time into complementary pairs until the world as we know it was conceived. Heaven and earth, man and woman, birth and death, day and night, light and dark, *yang* and *yin*. You may wonder why everything was paired in this way, but a single entity would have been insufficient. In the beginning, two became one, and from that union new life came. Whenever a single entity was paired with its opposite, the value of both became clear from the contrast – and the mutual association only enriched the meaning of both.

'Heaven was born from chaos, and so too was the earth. When heaven and earth divided, Ame-no-mi-naka-nushi, the Heavenly Centre deity, emerged on the Plain of High Heaven and rules at the heart of the heavens, exalted over all. Soon afterwards Takami-musuhi, the deity of Heavenly Creation, and Kamu-musuhi, the deity of Earthly Creation, were born. They are neither male nor female but are single, sexless deities, so neither appeared in a physical form.

'And what of the earth? Perhaps you are wondering what it was like at the time. Indeed, the earth floated upon the seas as formless as oil, bobbing through the waves like a jellyfish. Here, two gods came into being. The first was Umashi-ashi-kabi-hikoji, the esteemed deity of the Reed Shoots, who gives life to things by blowing upon them with a vital force. The other was Ame-no-toko-tachi, the Heavenly Eternal Standing deity, who guards the heavens for all eternity. Those gods protected the permanence of the heavens, and spur on the development of the earth below – their very existence points to the value of both. Neither Umashi-ashi-kabi-hikoji nor Ame-no-toko-tachi took a physical form. The five gods I have introduced, having neither body nor sex, are known as the Five Separate Heavenly Deities.

'The next gods to appear were Kuni-no-toko-tachi, the Earth Eternal Standing deity, who protects the earth for all eternity, and Toyokumono, Abundant Clouds Spirit deity, who possesses a force like roiling clouds, breathing life into all living things. These two as well are single, separate deities without physical form and no distinguishing sex.

'And then at last it was time for deities to appear in pairs of male and female. First came the male god Uhi-ji-ni and the female god Suhi-ji-ni, the Earth and Soil deities, who prepares the land so that it might sustain life. Next came the male god Tsu-no-gu-i or Horn Post deity, and his consort, the goddess Iku-gu-i, the Life Post deity. They give shape to life so that it might sprout upon the land. Next came the male Oo-to-no-ji and his consort Oo-to-no-be, the Great Door to Life deities. They determine whether the life forms henceforth created will be male or female. Next came the male Omo-daru and the female Aya-kashiko-ne – the Land is Perfected deities. They make the country fertile, prepare the human form, and encourage prosperity and fecundity.

'And then, Namima, who do you think came next?'

Izanami broke off her recitation to look at me.

'Izanami-sama and Izanaki-sama?'

'Indeed.' Izanami nodded. 'You see, the preparations had been very thorough and thoughtful. We were not thrust suddenly upon the earth. No. First, heaven and earth divided. And then, beginning with Ame-no-mi-naka-nushi, the Five Separate Heavenly Deities created and prepared the land below. Once that was done, two gods emerged from the five pairs of male–female deities. This pair was matched male to female like the others but they took a physical form so that they could produce children.'

'Izanami-sama, were you created to produce children?'

In my ignorance, I had been rude in asking that question. But earlier she had said there was a reason why I was her priestess, and now I had a vague idea of what it was. She was an exalted deity, but she was also female, and it had been her fate to couple with Izanaki and bear his children.

'That is not the only reason. I was also created to desire men, to love them. Izanaki and I were the gods of conjugal love.'

'But if that were so, why did you come alone to the Realm of the Dead? You said that Izanaki-sama had assumed a human shape, but where is he now?'

My questions pushed Izanami into a silence that dragged on and on, so long, in fact, that I was certain one growing cycle must have come and gone upon the earth. Sensing that I had offended her, I grew so anxious that I could hardly contain myself.

To my great relief, Izanami finally let out a long sigh, then resumed her narration.

'It will take time, but I will tell you what you wish to know. I am the archetypal desiring female, and Izanaki the desiring male. And, as my name suggests, I loved Izanaki. I invited him. And Izanaki for his part loved me. He invited me. Why, Namima? Why do you think we were created? Why did we *have* to love each other, to desire each other so much?'

'Was it so that you could give birth to children, Izanami-sama?'

'Yes. The first time we came together, we produced the land.'

'You gave birth to the land?' I parroted, startled.

'Certainly. We were gods. We gave birth to all manner of things. We created. The first order we received from the gods on the Plain of High Heaven was to solidify the land that had been drifting directionless upon the seas. We were to make it firm. We stepped out upon the floating bridge between heaven and earth and together thrust the spear we had received from above into the seas below us. We stirred the waters, and when we lifted the spear, the droplets that dripped from the tip congealed when they hit the salty waves below and formed an island. We named it Onogoro, descended from the heavens, and built ourselves a palace there. The palace was immense, far, far larger than the palace here. The main pillar was so tall it extended all the way to the Plain of High Heaven and allowed us to commune with the gods who resided above. We named it "the Pillar of Heaven".'

Izanami lifted her gaze upward, nostalgia sweeping over her face. I followed her eyes but I could not see the top of the pillar in our underworld palace. It disappeared into the looming darkness. As far as I could see, all was dark. It was as deep and impenetrable as a winter's night, as dense as lacquer. And we were imprisoned in it. I suddenly recalled the corpse that Mahito had thrown into the sea. My dead body had sunk to the bottom and nestled in the sand from the shoulders down. Fish had nibbled on my flesh. The last sight I remember – with the one eye that had been left to me – was of the darkness of the seabed. When I looked up now, in the palace, I remembered that last vision.

'Izanami-sama, if I may ask, it appears you were the first of the goddesses to assume the same form that we human women have. Is that so?'

Izanami's story had been interesting so far, but I could not forget my own situation, so I asked the question.

Izanami answered, 'It is. Our palace in Onogoro-shima was called the Yahiro-dono, or the Palace of Eight

Fathoms. Once we had built it, Izanaki asked, "How is your body formed?" You see, I was the first god to appear in female flesh, and Izanaki did not understand it. So I responded, "My body is perfect in form, but in one place it is empty." To this, Izanaki replied, "My body is perfect in form, but in one place there is excess." He continued, "Let me put my place of excess into your place of emptiness, and thereby fill it. In this way I should like us to give birth to the land. What say you?" And I agreed.'

As I listened to Izanami's account, I couldn't help but remember the first night I had lain with Mahito. The memory nearly took my breath away. I had had two older brothers, but they were so much older than I and had taken to the seas as soon as they came of age that I had had no idea what a man's body was like. The first time I saw Mahito naked, I was frightened but also fascinated by how different he was from myself.

I found myself wondering if perhaps Mahito was now in love with another woman. I was dead, so of course it made sense for him to be living with another woman. But I wouldn't have been dead if not for him. So to think of him now loving another woman filled me with bitterness. It was mean-spirited of me – and pathetic for the dead to feel such jealousy.

As I sank into silence, Izanami continued her story:

'Izanaki suggested that we circle the Pillar of Heaven. He went to the left and I to the right, and when I came upon him on the other side, without thinking I called with delight, "What a charming man I've met!" Apparently, Izanaki thought he should have been the one to speak first, but I had. Somewhat disappointed, he said to me, rather flustered, "What a charming woman I've met." And off we went, hand in hand, to the bedchamber in the palace and there we consummated our union. As a result, we gave birth to our first offspring. We called the bake Hiruko, or "Leech-child" because, like a leech, the infant had no bones and was limp and squashy. We placed the babe in a boat of reeds and floated it out to sea. The next child we had was the small island of Awa. We had meant to produce a great land, and a small island was hardly worthy of us. Something had gone wrong. We returned to the Plain of High Heaven to report to the gods there and seek their counsel.'

And then Izanami turned to me and asked, 'Namima, do you know what they instructed us to do?'

Of course, I had no idea and said as much. But I felt sorry for Izanami – to have gone through the pain of childbirth only to find that the child was without bones! I could not imagine her disappointment. It was tragic for the child, to be sure, but it was for Izanami that I felt pity. I had given birth to my first child aboard a tiny boat and only someone who has experienced pain like that can truly understand how she must have felt.

Izanami continued: 'The gods of the Plain of High Heaven said that when we circled the Pillar of Heaven I had spoken out of turn when I exclaimed, "What a charming man I've met!" before Izanaki had said anything. I was a woman, and women were not to speak first. They demanded that we return and do it again. So, Izanaki started to the left and I to the right, and when we met on the other side, Izanaki said, "Ah! Might this be a good woman?" and I replied, "Oh! Could this be a charming man?" And once again we lay together. The first child we produced from this union was the island of Awaji. Next we gave birth to the Shikoku and Oki islands. After that it was Kyûshû, and then the islands of Isa, Tsushima, and Sado. Finally we produced the largest island of them all, Honshû. Eight islands in all. We named the land we had created the Country of Eight Isles.'

For some reason it seemed as though Umihebi Island – the island of my birth – was not among those Izanami had borne. Well, it was a tiny island. And the islands Izanami had named were those that now formed what we knew as Yamato. In ancient days the islands were not so known because they were not all under the rule of Yamato. But I am getting ahead of Izanami's tale.

I remember in the few moments just before I died, I had caught sight of what looked like the large island of Yamato and had felt reassured. I wondered if Mahito and Yayoi were now living on Yamato. How happy I would be if they were living near Yomotsuhira-saka, the Yomi Slope. I wondered what kind of girl Yayoi had become. If she took after Mahito, she would have a lovely body. Perhaps she had a face like Kamikuu's – if she did, she would be far prettier than I had been. The more I thought of her, the more I grieved that I had not been able to tend to her myself.

'Namima, you are lost in thought. Are you thinking about the past?'

Because I detected disapproval in Izanami's tone, I pulled myself together and asked, 'Izanami-sama, what happened after you gave birth to the islands?'

Izanami did not answer immediately, causing me to wonder if perhaps she was tired of talking. But then she stared at me with those eyes that seemed to be looking at nothing.

'We had created the land. Next I gave birth to all manner of deities.' Her tone now was touched with gloom. 'The God of the Sea, the God of Water, the Wind

God, the Tree God, the Mountain God, the God of the Plains and then the God of Fire. But when I gave birth to him I was burnt so badly I died.'

I gasped, imagining how great the pain she must have endured. 'How agonising for you.'

Izanami nodded, somewhat annoyed. And then, out of the darkness, I heard the voice of a woman, low but unmistakable.

'Izanami-sama, you must be very tired. Shall I tell Namima the rest? It's the part you don't like. I will tell her all, and about Izanaki-sama, too.'

Without looking at the woman, Izanami settled into a low chair. 'I had thought to tell her the rest but suddenly I am feeling rather out of sorts.'

A woman appeared before us. She was short and her dress shabby. Although she looked frail, her voice resonated with surprising clarity and strength.

'I am Hieda no Are, descendant of Ame-no-uzume, the one known for her enticing dance at the entrance to the Heavenly Cave where long ago the Sun Goddess had sequestered herself. My skill is different. Whatever I hear, I never forget. Therefore, I have been entrusted with the honour of appearing before the emperor and recounting the creation of the world, from the age of the gods to the present. It was from my stories that

Oo no Yasumaro wrote his history. About that time, I fell victim to a pestilence and died an unhappy death. There was still so much left to do and my regrets were many. But now how delighted I am that my death led me to the Realm of the Dead where I can be of service to Izanami-sama.'

'Enough. Namima knows nothing of this so please start by resolving the many rumours.' Izanami had grown impatient.

Hieda no Are bowed and began to speak in a voice so melodious that her words flowed like water coursing over the earth after heavy rain.

6

'I, Hieda no Are, shall tell the tale of Izanami-sama and Izanaki-sama. The gods of male–female desire, Izanami-sama and Izanaki-sama were such a loving couple. Together they produced the land, the natural world, and the gods that there inhabit. And though they worked together as a couple, it was to the female deity, Izanami-sama, that the greatest burden fell.

'By that I mean, of course, that giving birth is dangerous – it can easily take one's life. And so it was that tragedy struck one day. Having given birth to much of the natural world, Izanami-sama finally gave birth to Kagutsuchi, the God of Fire, and in the process her female parts were badly burnt.

'As ill as she was Izanami-sama's desire to produce life did not falter, so from her vomit arose the male and female deities Kanayama-biko and Kanayama-bime. These two are the Deities of Mining. From her excrement sprang Haniyasu-biko and Haniyasu-bime, the Gods of Clay.

Next from her urine arose Mitsu-ha-no-me, the God of Gushing Water.

'All are related to fire. Because fire burns deep in the earth, the connection with mining is clear. As for clay, it takes fire to turn clay to pottery. And gushing water quells fire.

'And so, until the very end of her life, Izanami-sama concerned herself with giving birth to the land, the elements of nature and the gods that inhabit them — all that shapes this world of ours. Yet the wounds she received from the fire were such that eventually she died.

'When Izanaki-sama learnt that he had lost his beloved Izanami-sama, his grief was beyond description. She was his precious wife, so adored that no one could replace her, for they, being of kindred spirits, had together created the land. "O my beloved Izanami, my spouse, why have you died? I never dreamt that one of our children would deprive you of your precious life." Izanaki-sama cried before Izanami-sama's corpse. And then, furious, he began to writhe and wail. From his tears Nakisawame, the God of Springs, was born. Springs that flow ceaselessly with water now symbolise Izanaki-sama's endless grief.

'Izanaki-sama buried Izanami-sama on Mount Hiba. Once buried, Izanami-sama began her journey to the Realm of the Dead. But Izanaki-sama could not quell his grief. He had loved Izanami-sama too deeply to restrain himself. He was furious with Kagutsuchi, the Fire God who had inflicted Izanami-sama's mortal wound. He took the sword that was girded to his waist and, with a single stroke, cut off the god's head.

'Blood gushed from Kagutsuchi's body, drenching the blade of the sword and dripping to the ground. New deities sprang from each drop of blood. Of these, almost all were savage gods, among them the one who resides in the power of the sword strike, and another who represents the sharpness of the blade. The blood that had clung to the hilt dripped upon nearby crags, and from those drops were born the Gods of Thunder. Because it was the sword that had felled the God of Fire, the spiritual power of the sword is noticeably brilliant. Fire and the sword have an inseparable connection, do they not? The sword is born from fire, and the right to fire is controlled by the sword. Thus, the birth that took Izanami-sama's life delivered the new controlling force of the sword.

'Izanaki-sama dearly longed to see Izanami-sama. He set out in pursuit of her, following her to the Realm of the Dead, determined to find some way to restore her to the living. He travelled down Yomotsuhira-saka into the underworld. Presently he came to the Yomi Palace at the foot of the slope. He found the door locked but he knew his beloved Izanami-sama was on the other side, so he called to her. "My darling wife, the world that you and I have made together is still not finished. Hurry then, and return with me."

'When Izanami-sama heard him, she answered, "My darling husband, how I long to return with you. But you are too late, for I have already eaten food from the hearth of this realm so, as you know, I must now stay here. If only you had come sooner! Oh, how I loved you. And how delighted I am that you, my beloved husband, have come for me to this defiled world – even though you are too late. I want so much to return with you. Please wait here a bit. And promise me one thing – promise that you will not look upon me until I tell you that you may."

'All would be well when Izanami-sama returned so Izanaki-sama waited. He waited and waited but she did not come back. Eventually Izanaki-sama began to lose patience and, forgetting his promise, decided to search for her. When he pushed open the door to the Yomi Palace he found the interior so dark he could not see anything. His hair, parted in the middle and pulled into two knots atop his head, was decorated with combs. He took the comb from the left hair knot and broke out one of the teeth. He lit this with fire and, using it as a torch, went in search of Izanami-sama.

'Presently he heard what sounded like the rolling of thunder and he became aware of a horrible stench. Determined now to see what was there, he lifted his comb-tooth torch above his head, and saw Izanami-sama lying before him. What had become of her? His beautiful wife had changed completely. Her body was festering and squirming with maggots; her beautiful face had sunken into itself. The rolling he had heard was the sound of the maggots squirming. And on her face, her hands, her legs, on her stomach, her chest and her female parts, the thunder gods crouched and writhed. That is why it is taboo to carry only one source of light into a darkened room.

'Of course, when Izanaki-sama saw how Izanami-sama had changed, he turned to retreat. Once he did, Izanami-sama realised he had entered her room and shouted, "I told you not to look! You have brought shame upon me!" She then called for the strong women known as the Hags of Yomi and dispatched them to capture Izanaki-sama, who by now was fleeing through the long tunnel. The Hags set fast upon his heels so Izanaki-sama pulled one of the black cords that bound his hair and threw it behind him. As soon as the cord hit the ground it transformed into a bunch of dark grapes. When the Hags saw this, they stopped and fell upon the grapes, fighting one another to eat them.

'Izanaki-sama was thus able to put distance between himself and the Hags, but as soon as they had devoured the grapes, they were again upon him. This time Izanaki-sama pulled out the comb from the knot of hair on the right side of his head and threw it behind him. As soon as the comb hit the ground, the teeth turned into succulent bamboo shoots that burst up from the ground. When the Hags saw this, they sank their teeth into them and crunched greedily.

'Just when Izanaki-sama thought he had escaped, he saw that Izanami-sama had dispatched the eight Thunder Gods that had been residing on her body, accompanied by a fifteen-hundred strong horde of warriors. Izanaki-sama unsheathed his sword of ten spans and waved it behind him as he fled.

'When at last he came to the Yomi Slope, he picked three of the peaches that were growing along the side and hurled them behind him. At this, his pursuers turned and retreated.

'Seeing that her earlier attempts had failed to stop

him, Izanami-sama went herself in pursuit of her husband. When he saw this, Izanaki-sama took an enormous boulder, so large that not even a thousand men could move it, and rolled it in front of the entrance to the Yomotsuhira-saka, blocking it. He called in parting to Izanami-sama, "My beloved wife, Izanami! You are now the goddess of the Realm of the Dead, and we must go our separate ways. I hereby declare our divorce."

'But for Izanami-sama, on the other side of the boulder, separated from Izanaki-sama, the matter was far from settled. Because Izanaki-sama had been late to visit her, she had tasted the food prepared on the hearth in the Realm of the Dead and was ready to stay for ever in the underworld. Just as she had resigned herself to her fate, Izanaki-sama had appeared and seen her in her wretched state. She was so vexed by this turn of events that she answered, from the opposite side of the boulder, "My beloved Izanaki, your behaviour is reprehensible. You have trapped me in this place, and now you say you wish a divorce. From this day forward, therefore, I will take the lives of one thousand people each day in your land of the living."

'To this Izanaki-sama responded: "My beloved Izanami, you may do as you say, but I shall build fifteen hundred birthing huts and will daily see that fifteen hundred new lives are born."

'And that is why every day a thousand people inevitably meet their death, and fifteen hundred babies are born. Trapped by the great boulder, Izanami-sama became known as Yomotsu-ookami, the goddess of Yomi, the Realm of the Dead.'

Hieda no Are stopped and looked at Izanami. She had been talking as though she would never tire, and she might have continued, but she wanted to check first with Izanami, to gauge her reaction. Izanami's head was tilted to the side and she was gazing expressionlessly into space. I wondered if she were recalling the events of the past. What emotions did they evoke in her? But it was impossible to judge Izanami's feelings from her expression.

As for myself, I was shocked to learn how Izanami had come to select a thousand people to die every day. She had uttered her hateful challenge during the heat of her battle with Izanaki. Surely she had regretted it. But, far from regret, Izanami seemed to know only bitterness. She was angry with Izanaki for shaming her; angry with him for sealing her into the underground Realm of the Dead. And I had been brought here to assist her in her bitter enterprise of strangling the life out of those thousand people. I suddenly remembered the icy drop of water that had splashed upon my cheek and my heart froze.

Hieda no Are, oblivious to my thoughts, continued her account.

'Once Izanaki-sama had broken his troth with Izanami-sama, he returned to the Central Land of the Reed Plains and, looking towards the heavens, shouted, "I have been to a most foul place! I must wash my body and purify it at once!"

'He went to Himuka in Kyûshû. And there, at a river in a place known as Odo no Awaki-hara, he threw off all the garments he had been wearing and stood naked. From his cast-off clothing, his staff and his sack sprang sundry gods. And because among them there were gods that invited disaster, Izanaki-sama began washing to rid himself of all impurities. The current in the upper stream was too fast, and that in the lower was too slow. Izanaki-sama waded into the centre of the stream and dived into the current to scrub his body. From the filth that had attached itself to him while he was in the defiled land sprang two gods, Yaso-maga-tsuhi, the Abundant Misfortune Deity, and Oo-maga-tsuhi, the Deity of Great Calamity. They, too, are malevolent gods who invite danger. In order to right the evil those gods induced, Izanaki-sama washed again. And when he did, three more gods appeared: Kamu-naobi and Oo-naobi, the Great Rectifiers of Evil, and Izu-no-me, Consecrated Female Deity.

'Izanaki-sama dived to the bottom of the river and from his wake were born Soko-tsuwa-tatsumi, Water Spirit of the Deep, and Soko-tsu-tsu-no-o, Bottom Dwelling Lord. When he bathed in the centre of the stream, there came into existence Naka-tsuwa-tatsumi, Water Spirit of the Centre, and Naka-tsutsu-no-o, Centre Dwelling Lord. And when he returned to the surface of the water and rinsed himself, Ue-tsuwa-tatsumi, Water Spirit of the Surface, and Uwa-tsutsu-no-o, Surface Dwelling Lord, were born. These Wa-tatsumi gods are related to the waters and to the sea, and so are gods of the sea and are born of the sea.

'Once he had cleansed himself of the pollution of the Realm of the Dead, Izanaki-sama rinsed his left eye. A most beautiful goddess emerged. She was called Amaterasu, which means Goddess of the Sun, and that was what she was. When Izanaki-sama rinsed his right eye, he brought forth a splendid male deity, Tsuku-yomi. This name is written with the characters for "moon", *tsuki*, and reading, *yomu*, and means "to read by the light of the moon". He was the God of the Night Skies. And, finally, Izanaki-sama rinsed out his nose. When he did, a God of Great Valour was born, Take-haya-susano-o.

'As a result of the purifications Izanaki-sama performed upon his return from the underworld, he gave birth to three splendid offspring, and so he was greatly pleased. Among these, he was particularly impressed with Amaterasu, so he said, "I have continued to produce children for some time. These three are splendid so now I am satisfied."

'Then, with no warning, he took off his necklace – beautiful beads dangling – and placed it around Amaterasu's neck. He made of her a god above all other gods and named her to a position in the Plain of High Heaven where she would be in control of all. Tsuku-yomi he sent to rule the heavens of night. And Susa-no-o became the God of the Sea.

'Izanaki-sama had produced the land with Izanami-sama. How was it that he was able to produce god after god on his own? It is said that this power adhered to him because he had travelled to the Realm of the Dead. And when he gave birth to the radiantly beautiful Amaterasu, he felt that his work had reached its pinnacle. With an air of great contentment he said, "Herewith I have produced gods sufficient."

'However, Izanaki-sama had not forgotten the words uttered when he had broken his troth to Izanami-sama. If Izanami-sama was to take the life of a thousand people every day, he had to make good his promise to build fifteen hundred birthing huts. Izanaki-sama assumed the form of a human man and went about his resolve to create superior children. He heard that there were beautiful women in the region of Yamato so that was where he went, making every woman he encountered his wife. Presently, each of his beautiful wives delivered babies. In this way, Izanaki-sama counteracted Izanami-sama's wresting away of life by producing it.'

'That's enough!' Izanami interrupted.

Hieda no Are looked up at her and released a long sigh. For the first time she noticed that her monologue had put Izanami in a bad mood.

Izanaki's behaviour upon his return from the Realm of the Dead, after breaking his troth to his wife, had effected a complete denial of his earlier time with her. And his reference to her realm as a place of defilement hurt not only Izanami, but all the dead who were there, myself included. Moreover, even though the two deities had worked together to produce the land, Izanaki had wasted no time in relying exclusively on his own efforts to procreate. And when he had finished, he was effusive about the satisfaction he had derived from his ability to create glorious gods like Amaterasu and Tsuku-yomi.

Izanami was sealed into the defiled Realm of the Dead and humiliated because her husband had looked upon her festering, repulsive body. The shame was such that she lost all the dignity she once had known as the mother of the land. She had once been responsible for giving life. She had produced the land and many of the children on it – a responsibility she had happily shared with Izanaki. But now the mother of the land had become the bestower of death, with the daily task of taking the lives of a thousand. How horribly ironic!

I recalled Izanami's words: 'Heaven and earth, man and woman, birth and death, day and night, light and dark, *yang* and *yin*. You may wonder why everything was paired in this way, but a single entity would have been insufficient. In the beginning, two became one, and from that union new life came. Whenever a single entity was paired with its opposite, the value of both became clear from the contrast – and the mutual association enriched the meaning of both.'

But once Izanami had died, the value of the pairing was lost and she became associated only with the dark half: earth, woman, death, night, dark, *yin* and, yes, pollution. It might be presumptuous of me to suggest it, but what had happened to her was not unlike my own fate. On Umihebi Island, I had been assigned the role of *yin*, and was named 'impure'. I understood Izanami's anger and bitterness.

Izanami began to speak: 'Everything Hieda no Are has

said is true. Each day when I search out the thousand I will deprive of breath, the first ones I strangle are Izanaki's wives. You would think that when people see Izanaki approach they would know he invites disaster and run away to avoid him.'

Hieda no Are drew her thin brows into a frown. 'Izanami-sama, what you have said teems with cruelty.'

Izanami did not bother to look at her. 'Where is the cruelty? I am the one who was locked inside this place. Am I not the Goddess of the Underworld? Am I not then acquiescing to my fate?'

I could feel the black flame of anger emanating from Izanami's body. Instinctively, Hieda no Are and I fell to our knees and prostrated ourselves. A pall fell over the hall as if even the spirits who floated aimlessly through the palace were holding their breath.

'Well, Namima?'

Izanami was staring at me with her cold eyes. But I was too terrified to meet her gaze.

'Your anger is natural.' I spoke honestly. Of course, I also agreed with Hieda no Are. I thought it excessively cruel to kill Izanaki's wives and I worried about what such acts had done to Izanami's reputation. Even so, I knew exactly how she felt. Izanaki had gone on living his life, seeking out wives and having children with them, showing no concern for her. They had once acted together, producing the land. She had even given her life. And to what end? Who was looking after her now, defending her dignity? How must she feel when she thought of the husband she had loved so dearly? I vowed then and there to do whatever I could to help Izanami.

'Izanami-sama, I now understand why I am here. From now, I shall devote myself to you and your work.'

I spoke with all my heart, but Izanami's expression did not change. Saying nothing, she turned and walked out of the room where she worked – the room in which she determined each day which thousand people would die.

WITH ALL I DO IN THIS WORLD

1

It was Izanami's task to select who would die – a thousand people every day. And whenever she set about it, I was always at her side, waiting to serve her, silently watching as she scattered the drops of black water over the map. Human beings can't live for ever, of course, but many of those Izanami summoned unto death were still very young. Death came to them without warning. Most prominent among them were the women Izanaki took to wife. One after another they met an untimely end, surely triggering turmoil in the world of the living. I stood beside the map, watching, while the drama played itself out.

Izanami set her bowl of water on the floor unexpectedly and gave an anguished sigh. 'Namima, do you suppose the effort and pain I endured in creating the land and gods with Izanaki were all in vain?'

'Of course not! Izanami-sama, you laid the foundations for the creation of Yamato. Nothing you have done has been in vain.'

'Then why am I in such a place?' Izanami pointed at the endless darkness above her. Her sudden movement must have startled the spirits who drifted around us for I sensed them leaping wildly.

'Because upon your death you were sent to rule the underworld – you are its goddess.'

'That wasn't a decision I made for myself, though. And, besides, gods do not die.'

Izanami spoke with open bitterness, which was unusual for her. I held my tongue. Clearly I could not know who had determined Izanami's fate. Perhaps it had been decided by the highest of the gods dwelling in the Plain of High Heaven. I did know, though, how she felt. How easily I could understand her despair.

'Izanaki and I came together as a couple and we produced the land with great effort. Why is it that Izanaki alone is permitted to walk freely in the world of sunlight?' She collapsed upon her seat of granite, looking exhausted.

Desperate to cheer her, I said, 'Izanami-sama, it was childbirth that caused your death. There was nothing you could have done. And since Izanaki-sama is male, his life has never been so threatened. It was childbirth that decided the difference in your fates.'

But Izanami's anger did not abate. 'So you say, but male though he may be, Izanaki gave birth to all those other gods after he left the Realm of the Dead, did he not? And, as Hieda no Are related, he took great pleasure in having produced the highest-ranking god of all – the Sun Goddess, Amaterasu. What of the children I – the female deity – produced? Why was none worthy of becoming higher still? Was it because I was defiled and, as such, locked away in this underworld of death? Namima, can you understand how sad this goddess is? I am separated from the only man I have ever loved and forced to live among the dead while he, Izanaki, moves from one young wife to the next, producing new life again and again.' Izanami began to weep.

I could think of nothing to say so I hung my head. But to the very depths of my being I sympathised with her lament.

She continued with her task, silently and listlessly. Determining who would die was, in truth, a chore that left an unpleasant aftertaste. Once death was visited upon a person, they were torn cruelly from their loved ones and forced to confront it alone. Death is inescapable but to die unexpectedly is desperately sad. Surely those who received Izanami's death sentence became tormented spirits unable to slip quietly into the next life.

The underworld was full of disconsolate souls waiting helplessly in the darkness, their hearts tortured by regret as they thought, if only I'd known her summons would come so soon, I might have done this . . .

Izanami's work invited disaster and brought sorrow to many. In contrast, Izanaki built birthing huts that saw fifteen hundred new lives each day; his task brought great joy. The couple who had been so devoted to one another had been torn apart by her death and forced to travel along different paths. Why was that? I could tell from a glance at Izanami's dour face that she, too, was troubled by the same question.

'Izanami-sama, I must ask you something.' I had bided my time, and now I felt the moment was right.

'What is it that you wish to know, Namima?' Izanami took up the bowl and handed it to me.

Careful not to spill a drop, I clutched it, then set it carefully on the cold stone floor. 'Izanami-sama, how is it that you have information about the world of the living? You said earlier that you receive reports from the living and the dead. But I wasn't certain what you meant.'

Izanami smiled. It had been so long since I'd seen her smile that my heart leapt.

'You haven't noticed yet, Namima?'

'Noticed what?'

'Look over there.'

I had no idea what she was talking about. But I looked

nervously around the chamber while Izanami pointed here and there in the darkness.

'See? Flies.'

Sure enough, little flies were flitting through the darkness. So, tiny living creatures did visit the Realm of the Dead.

'They enter through the Yomotsuhira-saka. Snakes, flies, honey bees, black ants – all kinds of little creatures find their way in and give me news of the world beyond. Migratory birds spread the news to other birds; the birds tell the insects; and they come to me.'

I leant forward. 'So that is how you know about Izanaki-sama's doings!'

'I do. But Izanaki doesn't know that I know!'

Izanami's features hardened. Should I go on or not? I hesitated, then screwed up my resolve. 'Izanami-sama, do you suppose the insects would be able to tell you what has become of my husband and daughter?'

'I asked as soon as you arrived, Namima,' Izanami replied. 'A tiny winged insect told me.'

I was stunned. Did she mean they were dead? Were they here, floating about like those wispy spirits? Even though I hated him now, I still wanted to understand what Mahito had been thinking when he had done what he did. I wanted so much to see him again. 'My husband

and daughter are living on Yamato, aren't they?' I asked impatiently.

Izanami's answer surprised me. 'They are not on Yamato. Mahito returned to the island with your daughter.'

I couldn't believe my ears. Why would he have gone back after that long, arduous voyage? What had been the point of it? Had we sailed away only so that he could kill me? But our escape had not been for me alone. Hadn't we wanted to leave the island to spare our unborn daughter the cruel fate that awaited her there? We had risked everything to leave. It didn't make sense.

'Izanami-sama,' I began to plead, the tears falling down my cheeks, 'I want to know more, please. I'll suffer any punishment, pay any price, if I can just learn how they are.'

Izanami said nothing. Whenever she lapsed into silence, it might be a very long time before she spoke again. And the longer her silence, the more important what she had to say. I waited as patiently as I could until, at long last, she answered. 'There will be no punishment. But, Namima, even if you learn what you want to know about the living, you will not feel relieved.'

I nodded vigorously. 'I understand. I just want to know how Mahito and my daughter are faring.'

'You'd be better advised to relinquish this desire.'

'Why? You must know something you have not told me.'

Izanami shook her head. 'All I know is that they returned to the island – and I don't want to know more than that. The more we know about the living, the less we benefit. Those of us in the Realm of the Dead would be better to forget the living.'

I remembered what Hieda no Are had said. After Izanaki had parted from Izanami at the Yomotsuhira-saka, he had purified his body, claiming he had been in 'a defiled place'. When he had given birth to one god after another, he had been beside himself with joy. He had sought out human women, taken them to wife and produced children.

But those who existed in the Realm of the Dead were for ever defiled. It was the same for me. I gazed at Izanami, her dark expression, and knew I had to speak.

'Izanami-sama, now that I know my husband and daughter are on the island where I was born, I cannot contain myself. Even if it's just for a brief time, I want to return to the world of the living. I want to see them for myself.'

'There is one way that you can do this. Namima, you are not a god. You exist merely as a spirit. But if you will be transformed into a tiny fly or a maggot or some other such creature, you may leave.'

Earlier Izanami had said, 'That is not to say that there is no way out.' This must have been what she meant.

'I'll become an insect if it means I can leave.'

'Are you sure, Namima?' Izanami seemed eager to dissuade me. 'You cannot leave in human form. But is turning into a fly or a maggot to be welcomed? Whatever you saw when you were a human being, whatever you felt, will not be the same now. Human beings are not gods, after all.'

She seemed determined to test my resolve. I suppose she doubted that I had the courage to become such a disgusting creature.

She seemed to give way. 'Very well. But when the insect you become dies, you must return to the Realm of the Dead. Do you still wish to go? Of course, you will have no control over your death, or how you die. You may endure yet another agonising death.'

Izanami took up the bowl as she spoke and began to cast the remaining water on the centre of Yamato. Droplets splattered here and there with little order – and wherever they landed, people in Yamato died without warning. Many, many suddenly dying . . .

I left the chamber and wandered out into the dark

corridor. I wanted to see things with my own eyes, I had told myself. But once I had made my way back to the world of the living, it would be painful to leave it again and return to the Realm of the Dead. The more I thought about it, the more my resolve weakened. But, no, I had to see them. I had to know. I would show Izanami . . . Still, I was confused, my thoughts tangled and torn.

'How are you, Namima?'

Hieda no Are stepped out from the shadows of a massive pillar. Realising that her narrative had put Izanami in a bad mood, she had withdrawn from the goddess's presence. But I had enjoyed her stories. Speaking before exalted people was her task, and she was able to describe the age of the gods so vividly I had seen the stories unfolding before my eyes. And no matter how many times she told of the events, her narrative never varied, not by a phrase or even a word. When she told her stories, she made my dreary life in the Realm of the Dead almost enjoyable, if only for a short time.

'Namima, you seem upset.'

Hieda no Are was a head shorter than I and she had to crane her neck to look into my face. I was uncomfortable under her scrutiny, and turned away.

'Has something been troubling you since you came

to the palace? Did Izanami-sama scold you?' She took my hand in hers. We were both spirits and all but invisible, except for the faintest outline of a human form, so she could not squeeze my hand, but her power surged into me, making me start. She and I were the most insubstantial of existences – all emotion and awareness, little more – yet, surprisingly, at that moment I could feel the press of human flesh. I was overwhelmed by nostalgia. Life was so wonderful. And here I was, dead, locked in this horrible place, completely cut off from the world of the living. What should I do? I felt trapped by my uncertainty. Without thinking, I unburdened myself to Hieda no Are.

'Izanami-sama told me that my husband and daughter went back to the island after I died, and now I don't know what to do – the news upset me so much.'

'But, Namima, you're dead. Why does it matter? The living mourn the dead for a time but they forget about them as the days pass. The living are so selfish, so spoilt, so taken with the very act of living that they don't remember long. And why should it be any different with us? We have nothing to do with the living. Wouldn't it be better for you to let them go?'

She was clear in her conviction, but I could not share

it. Mahito and I had been so steadfast in our resolve and so determined to escape our fate on the island, but Hieda no Are had no family and had been loved only by the rulers of Yamato: she could not possibly have understood this.

'I regret not being able to help my daughter.'

This time she smiled and began to tease me. 'So you say . . . but, Namima, you're not just worried about your daughter, are you? It's your husband you can't forget! You were so young when you died, and you're worried that he is enjoying himself with another woman. Am I wrong?'

No. Dead though I may be, not a day goes by that I do not think of Mahito. There was just one thing I wanted to know. What had his true intentions been? My feelings were not much different from Izanami's when she thought of Izanaki. The living are arrogant. They live to pursue their own happiness. Of course, death awaits them, too. There's no escaping it. Izanami wanted to say to Izanaki: 'No matter what you do, at least don't deny what we accomplished together, or all the things we spoke about so earnestly to one another.' Now when I think of Mahito I feel the same doubts Izanami must feel. We had left the island at such enormous risk so why, after all that, had he gone back?

'With all I do in this world
Ne'er shall I forget
The lovely one who with me did sleep
On the isle where the wild ducks nest
Alighting from the offing . . .'

Hieda no Are explained that Ho-ori, known as Yama-sachi-hiko or Luck of the Mountain, had presented the poem to Toyo-tama, the princess of Watatsumi Palace. When the time came for her to bear Ho-ori's child, she turned into a crocodile. But she felt such shame because Ho-ori had seen her in that form that she left her child behind and returned to the Watatsumi Palace at the bottom of the sea. Far, far away though she was, she was unable to forget her child, so she sent her younger sister Princess Tama-yori to look after the child in her stead. This poem, Hieda no Are said, was the one Ho-ori wrote in reply to the one Princess Tama-yori had brought him from her elder sister.

'With all I do in this world/Ne'er shall I forget,' Ho-ori said in his poem, and I have not forgotten Mahito, even though my world ended. And just as Princess Toyo-tama pined for the child she left behind, I still worry for my Yayoi. How will she survive on Umihebi Island, with its cruel customs? The more I thought about the story, the more I wished I had a younger sister like Princess Tama-yori to whom I could entrust everything. But Kamikuu and I were worlds apart now, and I could not count on her to help me.

'Are-san, I am thinking of leaving the Realm of the Dead and returning to my island.'

'Can you do such a thing?' she asked in disbelief.

'Izanami-sama told me that I could if I were willing to change places with one of the tiny insects that slip in here along the Yomotsuhira-saka. Apparently a lot of insects enter there from the world of the living.'

Hieda no Are clapped her tiny hands in joy. 'I'll go too! I would like to see how the world has changed since I died. I wonder how I am thought of now – and what kind of funeral service I had! I will definitely go out to see.'

'But, Are, you can only do it once. And as soon as your insect dies, you have to return to the Realm of the Dead. Do you still want to go?'

'Yes, indeed. What do you plan to do, Namima?'

Once I had decided to go, I could not bear to linger in the Realm of the Dead a moment longer. Hieda no Are and I started off towards the Yomi Slope. Izanami was well aware of what we were up to. When we passed her chambers she called to us, though she did not come out to see us off. We left the palace and entered the dark, narrow tunnel. This was the pathway Izanaki had taken when Izanami, furious, had sent the Hags of Yomi to chase him down. But today the path was silent and still. There was no sign of another soul. We groped our way through the darkness without speaking.

Finally we saw a sliver of light far in the distance. We had reached the Yomotsuhira Slope. This was where Izanami had bade farewell for ever to Izanaki. And it was where I had lain after my death. I stared at the strong light filtering in from the land of the living and was overcome by a blinding thought. I wanted to return to the living. I didn't want to become an insect: I wanted another chance to live my life as a human being. I knew it was impossible, and my eyes welled with tears.

'Namima, you're wishing you didn't have to become an insect and could just begin your life again, aren't you?'

Hieda no Are's question came out in short gasps. She was ancient and the walk up the slope had left her short of breath. Terrified that Izanami might hear, I whispered, 'That's exactly what I was thinking.'

Hieda no Are was old enough to have been my

grandmother, and she spoke to me with pity. 'You were only sixteen when you lost your life so it is natural that you feel so. When I was sixteen, I had already entered service at court and had been invited to speak to any manner of exalted personage. Everyone said I was a child prodigy. When I was told something once, I committed it to memory so perfectly that it was as though I'd heard it a thousand times. No matter how long the story I was to recite, I never made a mistake.' She was filled with nostalgia.

'Are-san, when you came to this realm, where were you when you realised what had happened?'

She turned back and stared into the darkness. 'I was in front of the door to the palace. When I opened my eyes, I didn't understand why I was lying in such a dark place. I had fallen ill with a cold, you see, and my chest had hurt before I died. I had wanted to live longer to recite more stories, and I was beside myself with grief at not being able to do so. When I opened my eyes, I was filled with joy because I thought I was still alive. That was when Izanami-sama opened the huge palace door and called, "Are you Hieda no Are? You know the stories of the gods. I want to hear them all, every one." As soon as I saw her I knew she was Izanami-sama, and I was profoundly moved. I understood then that the stories I had told were all true. That's why I don't mind being here, even though I feel lonely at times. The task I have now is related to that which I did in the other world.'

As I listened to her, it dawned on me that I had not embraced my destiny as she had. I was born to be the priestess of the darkness so it had been my fate to enter Izanami's service. Now my desire to return to the world of the living and find out about my loved ones was so great that I was willing to become a maggot, or a snake that crawled through the dirt, or a cicada that, once it reached maturity, had but seven days to live.

'Look, Namima! It's an ant, a red ant. Ants are slow but they have long lives. I think I'll become an ant to see what has become of the world.' Hieda no Are kept her eyes fastened to the ground as she spoke. 'Namima, when we meet here again, I'll tell you all that I saw. Until then . . . take care.'

I had no idea how to transform myself into an ant, but before I knew it, Hieda no Are had disappeared. The tiny ant had reversed course and was crawling determinedly towards the light.

I did not want to become an ant and crawl along the ground. I had a sea to cross if I were to see Umihebi Island again. I couldn't transform into a bird, but at least I could become an insect that had wings and could fly. I stood before the giant boulder Izanaki had placed at the mouth of the cave. I shielded my eyes with a hand, peered into the ribbon of light and prayed. Before long I heard a loud buzzing, and when I looked closer I saw a large sparrow wasp, yellow with black stripes along its body. I'd never seen a wasp before, but it was fast and seemed strong . . .

2

As a wasp, I was able to slip through the slender crevice alongside the boulder and leave the cave. It had been so long since I had tasted fresh air. It was fragrant and seemingly boundless. Glad to be alive, I soared freely through the sky, deliriously happy. But a long journey lay ahead, I reminded myself, and slowed down to survey my surroundings.

Just as Izanami had said, a deep, jade-coloured sea stretched in front of the entrance to the Realm of the Dead. Rough waves rolled ashore one after another. I flew up and down the coast in search of a ship. But the only vessels moored along the nearby beach were small fishing boats. I couldn't afford to waste my time there, so I flew south where I hoped to find a larger port. Along the way I spotted a ripe melon that had fallen to the ground and split open. I stopped and ate greedily.

Now that I was a wasp, I had no idea of my lifespan, but in whatever time was allotted to me, I had to get home, to the Island of Sea Snakes. I had to find Mahito and Yayoi. I was too anxious to dawdle over eating. I didn't even have time to rest.

I flew for three days and three nights. On the morning of the fourth day I finally reached a large harbour far to the south of Yomotsuhira-saka. Exhausted, I landed on a tree trunk and surveyed the ships, searching for one that might sail towards the familiar chain of islands. I spotted one unloading white shells. It was a large vessel with white sails, large enough to hold more than thirty men. I'd never seen a ship like that near my island. Half-naked men were unloading huge crates filled with shellfish – wide-mouth conch, giant spider conch, and green turban shells, with their iridescent inner layers. The crates were so large it took a number of men to lift one. I was reminded of home. The shell of the wide-mouth conch was bright white and the meat inside thick and juicy. The only way to collect one was to dive to the ocean floor where it burrowed into the sand. The women on my island, who had trained themselves to hold their breath for a long time, would collect them and bring them to shore, as would the men who had been out to sea, fishing.

I had heard that the wide-mouth conch was used in fashioning bracelets and necklaces, but no one on my island took part in shell craft, and I had never seen them.

Mostly the shell was used for barter, and as soon as the men on the island had collected enough, they filled their ships with them and traded them for something else. I concluded that if I boarded the ship I had seen in the harbour, it would probably take me close to my island chain. I flew as quietly as I could towards it and fastened myself to the mast.

The following morning the ship set sail. I hid in the shadows of the cargo hold below so that I would not be blown away by the strong winds. Occasionally I would rest on the gunwales. Days went by and I had nothing to eat or drink.

'Hey, it's a yellow jacket! Kill it!'

Suddenly an oar came at me. I flew up in a panic and hovered over the surface of the ocean. My throat was parched so I flitted to the cask of drinking water.

'We've never had a yellow jacket aboard ship before.'

The sailors pointed at me, surprised that I did not fly off.

'Looks like it's got somewhere to go!'

There was a jokester among them.

'Well, if it stings you, you'll die. I'm going to kill it if it comes back.'

The man with the oar stood ready. For the first time I realised how dangerous humans were to a wasp. An older man, dressed in white, came over from the front of the ship to settle the crew down. 'That wasp might be a good-luck charm. If it comes back, leave it alone.'

Relieved, I flew back to the ship, which made the men laugh.

'That wasp understands us. If you promise not to sting anyone, you can ride with us. Fly in a circle if you agree.'

I flew in a circle. The sailors erupted in applause, then looked at one another, amazed. The man who had tried to kill me with the oar pointed at me. 'It might be our guardian deity for the voyage.'

I rested alongside the water cask and drank the water that the sailors spilt. Or I flew into the ship's pantry and preyed on the smaller insects there. Yellow jackets eat more than the nectar from flowers.

How many days and nights passed while I was aboard ship? Two weeks? More. The longer we sailed the ocean, the weaker I grew. Much longer and I would have died en route. I'd have had to return to the Realm of the Dead before I reached the island. I wanted to avoid that.

Two or three times strong winds buffeted the ship, and I was nearly blown out to sea as I struggled to fly below deck. Each time it happened the ship made for a small port, a group of islands or somewhere it could ride out the storm. If no port or inlet were to be found, the ship was tossed mercilessly on the high seas. My passage was anything but uneventful. I worried constantly: would I die before I reached my destination? The suspense was agonising. Even so, the voyage was much faster than the trip Mahito and I had taken on our little boat without a sail. On days when the winds came up, the ship glided over the waves as if it were flying. The boat Mahito and I had travelled on was beholden to the currents, and we had drifted with the waves.

One day the ship came to a large island with thick groves of trees. The sailors gingerly navigated into a lovely harbour with tall stands of chinquapin trees pressing down upon the shore and beaches of dazzling white sands.

I rested on the gunwale, surveying the scene, as boys and girls crowded noisily into the harbour. Waving their arms, they seemed delighted at the ship's arrival. Their faces were burnt black by the sun. Their eyebrows were thick, their eyes large – familiar features. Their garments, too, resembled those of my island in cut and pattern. Certain that I must be close to Umihebi Island, I flew off the ship.

'Look at that,' the ship captain pointed in my direction. 'The yellow jacket's leaving.'

'So, you were headed to the southern islands!'

'Good luck!'

The sailors waved me off with kind words of farewell. I flew circles in the sky to signal my gratitude.

I forgot the hardships of the long voyage. I was intoxicated by the scenery of the southern islands. During the languid heat of the early afternoon, the seaside morning glories nodded gently, beckoning insects. When night fell, the hibiscus changed from pink to beige and scattered on the ground. I flew back and forth nearly mad with joy to be among flowers I had not seen for so long. I sipped the nectar of the sweet naio and drank my fill of the dew on the camellia leaves. Then I flew through the dense thickets and soared towards the luxuriant mountains where I trapped and ate bugs and spiders and, finally, napped in the shade of a leaf. Wherever I looked there were vines and tangled thickets, lively insects, and sea serpents slithering over the dry sand.

Everything resembled my old home, but I was still not on Umihebi Island.

The next morning, my energy restored, I began to fly over the seas in the direction of the rising sun. Every time I neared an island I would slow to look, but none was Umihebi. Twice the sun rose and set as I flew, but I continued my flight east. Many were the times I was so exhausted that I thought I would die.

Gradually I came to understand that I was nearing the end of my life. No matter how I tried to encourage myself, I just could not find strength to fly on. I would die before I reached my island. Night had fallen, and as I skimmed over the surface of the waves, I remembered the cold darkness of the Realm of the Dead. A world with no colour, no scent. Here, in contrast, I was weary but I had the salty smell of the sea, the sweetness of the air, the night sky that went on and on for ever – such beauty and freedom that I would never have known had I not been alive. If I died now, all would be lost. I had to keep going. I had to see Mahito and Yayoi. Just a glimpse, just a glimpse, I chanted, to urge myself on.

Suddenly I saw a giant rock jutting out of the sea. I scrambled onto it and clung there. I did not know what island I was on or near, all I knew was that I could rest. I nestled into a tiny crevice and slept soundly.

The next morning when I woke I saw that pure white lilies bloomed along the rock. I'd seen this before. Wasn't this the northern coast where Mahito and I had set out on our voyage? I looked across the seas and saw the headland looming over the waves. The cape. There was no mistaking it. I could see its wall from the sea, but beautiful white lilies graced the crags and nodded gently as though welcoming the gods on their descent to the island.

Mahito and I, once we were far enough from land, had been so happy to have caught the currents that carried us from the island and launched us on our escape. We had taken each other's hands in celebration and just then, when we looked back to the island, the sight of the white lilies dotting the black crags was so beautiful it had taken our breath away.

And now at last it seemed I had returned to Umihebi. My life, I could tell, was ebbing. I imagined a wasp's span was at best a month. Before the light of my life went out, I had to find Mahito and my daughter. I wondered if I had time.

The island I had not seen for so long was precious to me. As I flew over the land and looked down at the pandan thickets, the sago palms and the clusters of fan palms, the tears poured in my heart. Beneath me I could now see the large boulder we called The Warning. From above, I could tell that it was at the very centre of the tear-shaped island, as if someone had driven a wedge through the middle.

I wondered if Kamikuu, Child of Gods, was well. She was now the great Oracle. Was our mother, Nisera, still alive? I didn't know how much time had elapsed since I'd been called to serve Izanami, and I wanted to see my family as soon as I could.

I headed in the direction of my house, flying fast. I didn't see anyone on the way. It was as if everyone on the island was dead. I saw no smoke rising from the houses, no women going out to work. But I had seen quite a few of the little boats, so distinctive to our island, crowding the southern port. Perhaps it was the time that the men returned from fishing.

If they were still living, my father and older brothers would have come home, too. I forgot that I was a wasp and my heart raced as it had when I was a little girl. I began looking here and there eagerly for signs of my family. The air smelt dry and briny; the sands glistened under the sun, so bright it was nearly blinding. And the surrounding limestone rocks seemed to sizzle with the heat. Succulent laurels covered the ground between the beaches and the houses. The island might have been poor, but it was rich with light and natural beauty. It teemed with life. I forgot about the cruel fate I had endured here and soared above, lost in a dream.

But the people, burnt black by the sun, had to work if they wanted to eat. Where were they?

Suddenly I came across a funeral procession. People were dressed in white and walked slowly side by side, just as they had when Mikura-sama died. But unlike Mikura-sama's funeral, all of the mourners were women.

And there was only one wooden coffin. It was not grand like the one that had contained my grandmother. But neither was it like Nami-no-ue-sama's coffin, plain and roughly hewn. Four robustly strong young men I had never seen before were carrying it, one at each corner.

Whose funeral was it? I couldn't imagine, and I was also startled by the style of the funeral, so unlike the one I had seen before. Spurring my exhausted body on, I darted this way and that.

There was a priestess at the head of the procession dressed in white. She had plaited strands of fern fronds circling her head, and two sprigs of yellow pandan blossom were thrust into either side of the headband, sticking up like horns. Her neck was encircled with strand after strand of pearls. She chanted and danced as she went, sounding a shell. She was a middle-aged woman with an impressive physique. She looked rather like Mikura-sama, but of course Mikura-sama was no longer alive. Unless I'd gone back in time. But was that possible?

> *Today, this very day*
> *Little priestess, thou hast hidden*
> *Fingers three in triangle pressed*
> *Upon the sands thrice obeisance*
> *The arc of the wave, the arch of the head*

Thou doth bow
Today, this very day
Little priestess rest in peace
The heavens welcome you
The seas lift you up
For this day, this very day
We offer our prayers

No. I'd thought it was Mikura-sama, but it was Kamikuu. She must have been in her mid-thirties. She looked exactly as Mikura-sama had when we were girls. No, not exactly. She was more beautiful than Mikura-sama. She was majestic. I do not know quite how to describe her womanliness in a way that others will understand.

Her face and arms were as white as snow – nothing short of a miracle on a southern island like ours, which took the full force of the sun. Her lustrous hair hung down her back to just below her hips, and her dark eyes had a commanding look. They were bright and confident as though imbued with the full and perfect happiness of life. And her voice rang like a clear bell that would entrance any who heard it. Her fingers were supple and graceful and she moved her feet in time with the rhythm of her chant. The hem of her white robe fluttered as she spun. It was hardly a prayer: she seemed to be in the midst of a dance. Mikura-sama had awed all who saw her with her dignity. But Kamikuu captured hearts with her beauty and vitality. Even though they were taking part in a funeral procession, everyone followed as though bewitched by Kamikuu's voice and movements.

I felt as if aeons had passed since I had last seen the island. Flustered, I scoured the surroundings for a familiar face. But other than Kamikuu, I didn't recognise anyone. Perhaps Yayoi was among the others. There were about ten young women at the end of the procession but none looked as though she might be Yayoi.

What if I had still been alive? I had adored my elder sister, and I was filled with joy at having seen her once more. I circled her, beating my wings. Her voice raised in song, Kamikuu suddenly looked at me.

'Kamikuu! It is your sister! Namima, Woman-Amid-the-Waves.'

I flew in circles in front of Kamikuu's face. Kamikuu, while clapping the shells with her right hand and jiggling her strands of pearls with the left, looked at me quizzically. 'Kamikuu, you are the great Oracle, a shaman, are you not? You understand what I'm saying, don't you? Please, please . . . it's Namima!'

I forgot that I had come to her from the underworld,

the Realm of the Dead and defilement. I buzzed my wings with all my might. Suddenly the shells in Kamikuu's hand flew into the air. I did not know what happened next. I fell to the side of the procession and lost consciousness.

When I came to my senses I felt lucky to be alive. I might have been trampled to death – or become a meal for a bird or a spider. I had even escaped being carried off by ants. For some time I had lain in the dirt, half dead. The sun was sinking and all around me it was growing dark. I tried to take flight, only to discover that my left wing was broken and crumpled against my belly. I had flown too close to Kamikuu, and she had hit me. I could not believe that the sister I had adored would hit me. The very thought of it broke my heart.

The funeral procession was long since gone and the ceremony at the Amiido would be over. I wondered who had become priestess of the darkness. But, more than that, who had died?

Kamikuu had been chanting 'little priestess'. I had to find out who the 'little priestess' had been. I had sworn never again to set foot in the Amiido, but I turned in that direction. I could not fly well. The damage to my wing was serious. I became all the more aware that my life was quickly drawing to an end.

I need one more day – even just half a day. Please! I

prayed to Izanami. I pictured her gazing into space with those unfocused eyes, pretending not to notice. And I was sure she was disappointed, even disgusted with me, at my willingness to pay such a price for one last look at the world of the living. But it had been my choice to change places with the sparrow wasp. I could have become an ant and lived a longer life. But I had chosen the wasp because it could fly long distances. So, if I died before seeing Mahito and Yayoi, I had no one but myself to blame. I sought out the soft female bloom of a sago palm and curled up inside, knowing that death would soon come.

I awoke the next morning with a start, jarred by a noisy butterfly. The late summer sun had not yet risen. By some stroke of luck, I was still alive. I started out once again in the direction of the Amiido in the furthest western corner of the island.

The rising sun dyed the round, grassy clearing of the Amiido red. Before me was the gaping opening to the white limestone cave. Twenty years must have passed since I was left there alone to open the lids of the coffins every morning, check Mikura-sama and Nami-no-ue-sama, console them and assist them in their passage to eternity. My fear rushed back to me vividly. And even though I was a sparrow wasp, my heart was pounding wildly.

The Amiido was the temporary abode of the dead. It was where the corpses lay, after the spirits had left. Of course, the crumbling coffins lining the cave were filled with the white bones of Mikura-sama, Nami-no-ue-sama and my ancestors. Some of the coffins were so deteriorated that bones poked out of them. In some cases, the coffins had broken open, leaving them exposed. Those closest to the entrance were the newest.

The roof of the tiny hut where I had once lived was freshly thatched with pandan leaves. It would withstand the heavy rain that fell every summer night and even strong storm winds. Resting in the shade of a white trumpet lily, I stared at the hut, coloured by the rays of the morning sun.

The door opened and a girl stepped out. The priestess of the darkness. Her presence was indispensable to the island, but it was tragic that she had been born to such a fate. Her eyes were swollen with tears. She let out a long sigh. I felt as if I were looking at my past self. I had been too frightened to enter the hut on my first night in the Amiido. This girl seemed more resigned to her fate than I had been. Perhaps she had been told from when she was a little girl that she would become the next priestess of the darkness. Her little body was rail thin, but her arms and legs were long and agile and she looked strong.

She seemed to waver before turning towards the cave. She went inside, loosened the lid of the newest coffin and peered in. She began her terrifying task. 'Good morning, Mother.'

The morning sun glittered off the tears that were rolling down her cheeks. Was the dead person the little priestess's mother? I drew closer, careful not to make too much noise with my wings. I looked over the girl's shoulder into the coffin below. The dead woman was old, her hair white. Her eyes were closed, her face peaceful.

'Mother, I will now do all the things that you were accustomed to do. But my first task is to send you on your way. It makes me so sad.'

The girl clung to the coffin, tears rolling down her cheeks. She wiped them with her palms. Her face, very lovely, was somehow familiar to me. But I couldn't quite place her. And I assumed from what she had said that the old woman in the coffin had been the priestess of the darkness, but that did not make sense. In my time, Mikura-sama and Nami-no-ue-sama had been a pair – one day, the other night. They had been sisters. One had tended the world of the living, the other the world of the dead.

'But, thanks to you, I'm not as scared as I might have been, Mother. Even if your body starts to fester, I won't

be frightened. Of course I love you, Mother. You were
so good to me. Now it's my turn to care for you. I'll
watch over you until the twenty-nine days have passed,
and you've turned into a spirit and have travelled to the
bottom of the sea.'

I can still remember that moonlit evening. Mikura-
sama and Nami-no-ue-sama appeared before me in their
living bodies to offer me their thanks. But I did not
deserve their gratitude. I had betrayed them. I was
carrying a child in my belly.

The girl spoke bravely: 'Mother, Nisera-sama is here,
too – she was always so kind to me and my older brothers.
They're here so I'm not afraid. And, besides, you did the
work before me. I'm ready. It makes me sad and lonely,
but someone has to do it. It can't be helped.'

Nisera? So my mother had died and been left here as
well? Her body had been laid somewhere inside the cave.
I felt a wave of sharp disappointment knowing that now
I would not see her again. But if she came to the underworld, to the Realm of the Dead, it wouldn't be so lonely
there.

The girl placed the lid back on the coffin, put her
hands together and bowed her head in prayer. She stood
and walked towards the cave entrance. On the night when
I'd become the priestess of the darkness my father and

brothers had placed a gate at the opening to the Amiido and locked me in. There was a gate there now as well. But it wasn't made of pandan thorns, as it had been when I was shut in. It was a gate in name only, made with plaited fern fronds.

On the other side of the gate I noticed a tall man leaning forward. His coppery skin stood out against the white mourning robes he was wearing, making his sturdy body all the more striking. Who was he? I'd seen him before. It couldn't be Mahito, could it? He was opening his mouth to speak. I pricked up my ears.

'Yayoi, are you all right?'

Shocked, I peered into the face of the girl. It was my daughter, she who was born in 'the deep of night'. I could see it now. Her face was like my mother Nisera's. And her long, thin body was like mine. The strength in her eyes reminded me of Kamikuu. No, I suppose they were more like Mahito's. His eyes had always been so full of purpose. The closer I looked, the more I knew she was my daughter, the most beautiful girl in the world. But why had Yayoi become the priestess of the darkness? I had been *yin*, so she would be *yang*.

Yayoi ran happily towards the man. 'Elder Brother Mahito! You came, just as you promised you would!'

So, it *was* Mahito. I stared at his face. His eyes had

the same intense look; his nose the same high bridge. His body had transformed into that of a sturdy seafaring man. But he still had about him the gentleness and generosity of his youth. I was mad with joy. Finally, I had found my husband and daughter! But why had Yayoi called the old woman, 'Mother'? And Mahito 'Elder Brother'? I flew round and round, buzzing. Mahito glared in my direction and made as if to swat me.

'That's odd,' he said. 'We don't have wasps on the island. And this one is big and probably spiteful. Be careful, Yayoi.'

Yayoi followed my flight with her eye. 'I'm so lonely here, I'm glad of any company – even a wasp's!'

I felt as though I'd been stabbed through the heart. I wanted more than anything to have human form so that I could speak to Yayoi. I wanted to tell her that I was her mother, that I had escaped from the island all those years ago to save her life. And why was she here anyway?

As if nothing were amiss, Mahito handed her something wrapped in a palm leaf. 'Your dinner.'

Yayoi took the packet from him. 'Elder Brother, Mother doesn't look dead. She looks as though she is sleeping. Would you like to see her?'

Mahito remained silent. He raised his hands to block the morning sun. With their large knuckles, they were beautiful. Those were the firm hands that had squeezed my own on the stormy night so long ago when I was coming back from delivering Kamikuu's food. Hands that had explored my body and uncovered the secret wick of my pleasure. On nights when I could not sleep, those were the large hands that had covered my eyes – and the hands that had been wrapped around my throat, hands upon which the sea-snake broth had spilt. I stared at the hands now bathed in the rays of the morning sun and grew wild with doubt.

Had Mahito passed off Yayoi as his younger sister? If so, the woman in the coffin was his mother. Her family, the Umigame, was cursed because she had not been able to fulfil her duty and provide the island with the substitute *miko*.

Mahito had returned to the island with the infant Yayoi and had deceived the islanders into believing that his mother had finally given birth to a baby girl. That meant he, his parents and younger brothers had been spared certain death. Mahito's mother was the auxiliary *miko* so she had become the priestess of the darkness when I had escaped from the island. It was the role of her family to fill the vacancy. And that meant, when Kamikuu, the great Oracle died, my daughter Yayoi would be required to follow her in death.

'Please don't ask me to do such a thing. You know it's bad luck for a fisherman to meet the dead in daylight. If I went to look at Mother I'd be breaking the rules and I'd invite punishment.' Mahito knitted his brows and looked around him worriedly. I was furious. He and I had broken rule after rule, hadn't we? How many times had the two of us eaten the food Kamikuu had left – food I should have thrown over the cliff into the sea? And what about all the times we had made love? I was supposed to remain a lifelong virgin. But I had become pregnant and we had fled the island. After all the rules we had broken, who would be punished? Only Yayoi. My heart felt as if it were going to break in two.

What should I do? I flew round and round, buzzing. Of course, Yayoi was innocent and unaware of any of this. She was just doing her best to fulfil the role she thought was hers.

'Elder Brother, when do you set sail?' she asked anxiously.

'Tonight. My son will bring your meals.'

'Thank you.'

'I almost forgot – use this.'

Mahito pulled a spoon from within the breast of his robe and handed it to Yayoi. It was made of turban shell. Wasn't that the spoon that Nami-no-ue-sama had used when she lived in the little Amiido hut? The night that Mahito and

I fled, it was the only thing I had taken with me.

'What is it?' Yayoi asked, as she gazed at it.

Mahito hesitated before he replied. 'It's something that a woman named Nami-no-ue-sama used. It was left with me.'

'Oh, I know why! She was the priestess before Mother took over.'

Neither of them had made any mention of me. I wondered why. And why hadn't Mahito told his daughter the truth? Namima was the priestess to follow Nami-no-ue. She was your mother. But Mahito spoke so easily with Yayoi, as if she were someone else entirely.

'Yes. And now it belongs to you, Yayoi. Use it in your little hut.'

'Thank you for your kindness.'

Mahito gave her hand a squeeze. 'You'll be lonely at first. But concentrate on your duties. When the funerary rites are over, the spirits will return to see you. So, please, do your best to see Mother off to the next life. She suffered long and hard to give birth to you.'

'I will. And you be careful, too, Elder Brother. How is Kamikuu-sama?'

'She's well.'

'I won't be able to see her for some time. Please give her my regards.'

'I will.' Mahito flashed his white teeth as he smiled. I landed on his back, so quietly he did not notice.

A handsome man in his prime, Mahito strode briskly along the island paths as I clung to him. Whenever he chanced to meet someone along the way, they would gaze up at him with deep respect, almost as if they were dazzled, and would greet him with a deep bow. What a contrast with the days when his family was cursed because it had failed to produce a female child. Mahito had not been allowed to join the other men on the fishing vessels but had had to go out with the women to pick seaweed and shellfish from the beaches. Those humiliating days were now over. And all because he had lied to the island chief and presented my daughter as his younger sister. My heart was filled with the blackest suspicion.

Mahito entered a tiny hut on the edge of the Kyoido. It was in the same place where Mikura-sama had had her cottage – where I used to leave the basket of food for Kamikuu. But Mikura-sama's cottage was no longer standing. Now there was a new house with a roof of pandan thatch and high, stilted flooring that gave it a pleasantly cool appearance.

Two youths were standing in front of the well in the

garden, binding coral to a heavy fishing net. They turned
and waved to Mahito. One boy was nearly full-grown and
had the build of a fine fisherman. The other was probably
around eight years old. Like his older brother, he looked
a clever boy.

'Welcome back, Father!'

Mahito nodded, and asked, 'Where is your mother?'

'She's at the altar, offering prayers for the safety of
the fishing fleet,' the older boy answered. The younger
looked at his father with bashful delight, then turned
back to repairing the net. Mahito patted his shoulder,
then strode off towards the altar. So, Mahito had married
Kamikuu and together they had had all these children.
Next a young girl of about sixteen came out of the house,
a little girl of about five at her side.

'Welcome home, Father!'

A daughter. The household of the great Oracle was
secure. Kamikuu had fulfilled her duties well. Splendid
and dignified as a *miko*, successful as a mother – and she
had Mahito's love.

I remembered how, long ago, she had confessed her
desire for him. 'I shall soon begin to have babies. That
is my fate. If I could have a baby with a man like Mahito,
I would be happy. But Mikura-sama told me I can't so
long as Mahito's family is under a curse.'

That was why Mahito had turned back so close to Yamato. He had to fulfil Kamikuu's desire. *I wanted to pray for my sister's happiness, and the happiness of my former husband. But I could never forgive Mahito for changing my daughter's fate.*

Still unaware that I was clinging to his back, Mahito walked towards the altar nestled in a grove of banyan trees at the centre of the Kyoido. Kamikuu, dressed in white, was standing there, facing east, earnestly at her prayers. Mahito waited patiently until she had finished. The words she chanted were the ones Mikura-sama had intoned. I vaguely remembered them.

> *Heavens . . . we bow before you.*
> *Seas . . . we bow before you.*
> *Island . . . for you we pray.*
> *Heaven-racing sun, revering you,*
> *Sea-bed creeping sun, shunning you,*
> *Our men sing the seven songs.*
> *Our men spell the three verses upon the waves.*
> *Heavens . . . we bow before you.*
> *Seas . . . we bow before you.*
> *Island . . . upon you we rely.*

Kamikuu turned, sensing Mahito's presence.

'Kamikuu,' he called.

Still in her prayer clothes, she flew into his arms. 'I don't want to be without you for so long.'

'It can't be helped. A man has to go to sea.'

'Promise me you'll come home safely, Mahito.'

'Your prayers will protect me.'

They remained in each other's arms, silent. It was clear that they were in love. I couldn't bear to look at them. Without a sound I flew into the banyan tree and landed on a root. Kamikuu raised her face to Mahito. 'If my prayers reach the heavens, I will keep praying until I die.'

'If you die, Kamikuu, the island will perish.' He buried his face in the nape of her neck as he spoke.

'When your mother died she seemed to know that you would be safely reinstated. She was a true *miko* after all. And she gave us such a wonderful replacement in Yayoi. I'm sure she died peacefully. But Yayoi will not be able to have children so there will be no alternative *miko*.'

Kamikuu looked up at Mahito with pity in her eyes.

'It can't be helped, Kamikuu. You must live a long life. We'll wait for a granddaughter. That's the island rule, isn't it?'

Now Mahito was willing to accept the fate the island imposed on him. That was why he had killed me — I had been in the way. When I understood this, the shock was almost overwhelming. He and I had waged a battle against the cruel fates that had faced us. Mahito had secretly carried Kamikuu's leftover food to his mother. And when she had failed to deliver a girl child, he had shared the food with me and had made me with child, priestess of the darkness though I was. Then we had fled the island. He had broken all the island rules with me. And now he had offered up my daughter to those rules.

'Mahito, even when you're away for the briefest time I am lonely.' Kamikuu rubbed her cheek against his. 'I've been in love with you ever since I was a little girl. I told myself, "If I can't have Mahito for my husband, I don't want anyone."'

'I felt the same way.' Mahito drew her close. 'How wildly I've adored you, Kamikuu – for as long as I can remember. But since my family was cursed and out of favour, I could only think of you as a precious pearl I must never touch.'

Never once in their conversations did I hear my name. Kamikuu's little sister who had died so long ago. The priestess of the darkness who had disappeared. That little scrap of a girl no one remembered. That was me. And now the sparrow wasp I had become trembled with fury.

'I was so happy when your mother gave birth to Yayoi. I had heard nothing about you for so long and I was worried.'

'Well, my mother was ill.'

'And then Namima jumped into the sea and drowned. Being the priestess of the darkness must have been more than she could bear.'

'She refused to accept her fate.'

When I heard Mahito say that, I summoned all the strength I had left and leapt into flight. I hovered right in front of his face. When Kamikuu saw me, her expression darkened. 'I saw that wasp yesterday. I thought I'd slapped it away.'

'It was at the Amiido, too – and we don't have wasps on this island. It must be dangerous.'

As Mahito reached out to kill me, I sank my sting between his brows, crying out, 'Liar!'

A look of utter shock spread over his face, as if he had heard what I had said, and then he collapsed on the ground. Kamikuu screamed. And I, in the midst of my rage, breathed my last.

3

I was lying in front of the door to the underground palace. I had returned to the cold black Realm of the Dead and the contrast it made with sun-drenched Umihebi Island was stark. It was just as Izanami had said it would be. And should she ask me if I were disappointed, I would have to answer that I was. Mahito's fickleness and betrayal had left ice in my heart. I felt that the Realm of the Dead was a suitable place for me now.

'Welcome home, Namima.' Izanami pushed the door open and stood before me.

I pulled myself to my feet and bowed. 'Thank you. Seeing the world of the living has calmed me, Izanami-sama. Thank you with all my heart for allowing me to go.'

'Namima, that was a heartless thing to say!' Izanami gave a bitter laugh. 'Those who have seen the radiant beauty of life should find it a little more painful to return here.'

'No, Izanami-sama. My experience has taught me a

valuable lesson. You told me that it was better not to know what happens to the living after we die. I did not understand the wisdom of your words then. But now I do. I have been naïve. From now I will serve you with the utmost trust and sincerity. So, please, think well of me.'

Izanami nodded her approval. Then she opened wide the two outward-swinging doors into the underground palace. 'Come in, please, Namima. I have a surprise for you.'

My head tilted to the side in curiosity, I followed Izanami along the corridor lined with the immense pillars. Ahead I saw a tall man dressed in white standing in the shadows. I halted. The prospect of looking at him was so disgusting to me that I could not make myself move any closer.

'What is the matter, Namima?' Izanami turned back to me. 'It's Mahito, isn't it?'

'Why is he here? Izanami-sama, did you bestow upon him one of your droplets of death?' I prostrated myself at her feet.

'What are you talking about?' Izanami spoke softly. '*You* killed him.'

I raised my head in disbelief. When I was a wasp, I had stung him between the eyes. Had that caused his death? Now Kamikuu and the children were alone. What had I done? 'Was it my sting, Izanami-sama?'

'Yes. The poison of the sparrow wasp is powerful. Normally Mahito's spirit would have been set adrift. But it seems he died with regrets so he is here in his living form.' She retreated into her chamber.

Mahito looked as if he did not know what to do with himself. He gazed forlornly at the ceiling, which melted into the darkness.

'Mahito.'

When he heard me call his name, he shifted his gaze in my direction. His face betrayed no emotion.

'It's Namima. Don't you remember me?'

'Namima?' Mahito stared at me blankly and shook his head. 'I feel I've heard the name before, but I can't remember where. I'm sorry.'

He turned to stare in the other direction, a confused, forsaken look on his face.

'I was your wife. I gave birth to your daughter aboard ship. We called her Yayoi. After that, you killed me. And I found myself here.'

How could he *not* remember me? His response had so shocked me my head began to reel, and it was all I could do to stop myself screaming at him.

But Mahito just shook his head again. 'When was that?

And you say I killed you? Are you sure? I don't remember any of it. And, besides, Yayoi is my younger sister.'

'No, she's not. She's our daughter – yours and mine. And I'm Kamikuu's younger sister. I was the priestess of the darkness.'

Mahito did not register even the slightest remembrance. 'Kamikuu is my wife, the priestess of light. But the priestess of the darkness was Nami-no-ue-sama.'

'And Namima followed Nami-no-ue-sama. You came to see me often while I was in the Amiido.'

Mahito wasn't listening to me now. 'Where is this place? And why am I here by myself?'

'This is the Realm of the Dead. And you're here because you're dead.'

'I'm dead? But Kamikuu was praying for me. She was to make sure I came home safely.'

Mahito sank dejectedly upon one of the cold palace stones. He must have thought he had died while he was at sea, fishing. Struck by the futility of our exchange, I left the hall. I didn't exist in Mahito's memories. Did this mean my own memories of having loved him were now just adrift in space? It seemed reasonable that they would disappear along with my past. Did that mean I didn't exist anywhere? That I never had? If so, there would be no point in begging him to forgive me for killing him. My spirits sank deep into the gloom of the under-world palace.

Wilful and proud, did I envy Izanami her task of selecting a thousand people each day to die? Was that why I had killed Mahito with my poisonous sting? How I had loved him, even after he had killed me. But Mahito — insubstantial spirit that he was — was himself still in love with Kamikuu. Separated from her now for all eternity — all that was left for him was to become an empty drifting spirit, never to be free of his earthly desires. Knowing this meant that peace for me, too, was impossible.

And now I knew of one other kind of emptiness. I had assumed that my bitterness and anger would evaporate as soon as I had killed Mahito. But once the spark of bitterness is lit, it is difficult to extinguish. Even with Mahito as dejected as he was, the flame of my bitterness still flickered. Did I have no choice but to suffer?

Izanami had said that humans were not gods. How then could she understand the torment of my feelings? I wandered purposelessly along the corridor until I found myself in front of the chamber into which Izanami had disappeared. The door was closed. Like Izanami's heart.

HOW COMELY NOW THE WOMAN

1

Its sails filled with wind, the ship cut through the waves at a vigorous clip. Yakinahiko, a white goshawk perched on his right arm, took a position at the bow, his eye on the course ahead. His young attendant, Unashi, stood at his side. The sailors scrambled along the deck and glanced from time to time at Yakinahiko, who seemed relieved finally to have wind in the sails. Standing there with his goshawk, he looked like the God of Safe Passage.

The wind was steady and the ship picked up speed, slipping quickly over the vast sea. The creaking of the mast, sounding eerily like a series of shrieks, kept up a constant din. The goshawk faced the wind head on and puffed out his chest as if about to take flight.

'Sailing invigorates one, doesn't it, Unashi?' Yakinahiko stroked the goshawk's sharp beak.

Unashi had been seasick, his face still pale with nausea. But he seemed at last to have found his sea legs. A bright smile played about his lips as he turned to his master. 'If it stays like this, I think I could sail for ever.' His eyes

shone with respect for his master. Yakinahiko was thirty
and in the prime of his manhood. His countenance was
noble, his complexion fair, and his height well over six
feet. His arms and legs were long, his chest broad, and
his hair – parted in the middle and bunched into knots
just above each ear – was thick and black. Unashi, in
contrast, was nineteen and a mere slip of a lad. His body,
not yet filled out, was willowy, and his face still bore a
boyish trace, which lent him a forlorn air. The two might
have been mistaken for brothers, separated by a few years.
They were off, with the goshawk Ketamaru, on a journey
that had no clear destination, stopping along the way to
enjoy a hunt when the opportunity arose.

Yakinahiko usually travelled on horseback. This was
only the second time he had boarded a shellfish trawler.
The first time had been about a year earlier. He had felt
like taking to the seas, having come across men with shell
armlets. That would have been in a village towards the
southern end of Yamato. Almost all its inhabitants decorated their bodies with shell ornaments. The women and
children wore small bracelets on their left wrists and the
men encircled their right biceps with shells that had once
contained a thick white meat.

When Yakinahiko had entered the village he had been
on horseback, his attendant Unashi following fast on foot.

The villagers had gathered around them. At first the menfolk had been intimidated by his bow and arrows and his long sword; when they had glimpsed the jade jewels strung around his neck, they had shrunk back. Jewels were a mark of nobility and recognised as such throughout all of Yamato. The women, on the other hand, had been pleasantly surprised to see two such attractive men and sighed audibly over the luxury of their white silk garments. The children, driven by curiosity, had wanted to tease Ketamaru, and when they had tried to touch Yakinahiko's long sword, Unashi had had to scold them.

'What is the shell you wear about your arm?' Yakinahiko had asked.

A man in his early forties pushed through the crowd and answered respectfully. 'The bands are fashioned from the wide-mouth conch. The ones the women and children wear are made of the smaller cone shell. People like us make our living mostly from the crops we raise, so water is vital. That is why those who bring rain are exalted, and they wear the rarest shells of all. In this village, I bring the rain.'

The man had spoken with a touch of pride. He must have been the local shaman. The shaman had slipped the shell armlet over his wrist and handed it to Yakinahiko.

It was heavy and carved on the outer side in a beautiful pattern.

'The craftsmanship is very fine,' Yakinahiko had noted, with admiration. 'Where did you acquire this?'

'Far across the seas there is a chain of islands where they collect these shells. We go back and forth in ships to barter our grains and pottery for the jewellery they fashion from the shells.'

This had surprised Yakinahiko and he glanced at Unashi. Unashi shook his head slowly. Apparently he, too, was hearing of these islands for the first time. The two had travelled to every nook and cranny of the kingdom of Yamato, but they had never heard of a chain of islands across the sea so they had never ventured that far.

'Where is this island chain?'

'It is due south as far as you can go. The seas there are full of little islands all strung together. You can travel easily from island to island because the sea is not difficult to navigate. The island furthest to the south looks nothing like Yamato. I hear it is very beautiful but the poison there is unlike anything we have here.'

'Poison? What kind of poison?'

The shaman had grinned. 'I couldn't say. But you can be sure that in a place where everything is beautiful there must be people, plants or animals that carry some trap or poison that's too horrible for us to even imagine. That's what people mean when they talk about the poison there.'

Yakinahiko had determined that he would travel to that distant island chain. He wanted an armlet like the one the shaman wore, but more than that, if he went somewhere he'd never yet been, he might discover women more beautiful than any he'd ever seen. The notion had stirred him and he could not quell his excitement. The prospect of encountering an unknown poison had sent a shiver up his spine.

Driven by curiosity, Yakinahiko had boarded a swift-sailing shellfish trawler and journeyed upon the seas for two weeks before making port at Amaromi, the large island at the entrance to the chain. There, he had met Masago, the beautiful daughter of the island chief, and had made her his wife.

That had been a year ago. Now he was sailing home to his island princess. Around his right arm, hidden beneath his sleeve, he wore the armlet fashioned of wide-mouth conch that Masago had given him. The radiance of the shell and its exquisite craftsmanship were even more impressive than they had seemed on the shaman's armlet. Yakinahiko touched the armlet under his garment with his left hand. He had missed Masago. He had never felt such longing for any other woman who had become his wife . . . No, perhaps there had been one other in the past, long, long ago. Then he had been nearly mad with desire for his wife. He recalled having wanted her so badly he almost preferred death over the agony of his desire. But he had lived so long, as long as a boulder, and had now forgotten it.

'Yakinahiko-sama, what's that?' Unashi pointed to something just ahead of the ship. It was a small, reed-woven boat, bobbing up and down on the white-capped waves. Whenever one of the waves broke over the craft, it seemed likely to sink but then it would right itself again, rising and falling with the waves.

For some reason Yakinahiko's heart began to pound. 'I've never seen anything like it.'

Unashi looked anxious.

'Call someone to us. I want to ask about it.'

Unashi clambered over the pitching deck and shouted to the helmsman.

Summoned before the nobleman, the sailor pros-trated himself at Yakinahiko's feet. Yakinahiko pointed to the reed boat and asked, 'Why is that little boat out there?'

The helmsman raised his head. When he caught sight of the boat his face froze. 'It carries the body of a dead infant. In the islands around here, when a child dies at birth the parents put it in a little reed boat like that and float it out to sea. They pray for the boat to carry the child to the peaceful kingdom on the other side of the sea where it will be given a new life so it can come back again.'

Yakinahiko looked at the tiny boat. It was sinking. There was a tug at his heart. At some point in the past he had set a little reed boat afloat on the seas. His mind raced. But when? And with whom? He could not remember. He was certain he had. But had he? His memory was too hazy to be trusted. Several hundreds of years had passed since Yakinahiko had assumed the guise of a man, a human. No, several thousand. Originally he had been a god, a male deity, but so long ago that he could scarcely remember it.

'To meet the pain of parting after enduring the pain of childbirth . . .'

The helmsman heard what Yakinahiko had murmured and lowered his forehead with a look of compassion. Yakinahiko tended to feel things more deeply than most, and when he put his feelings into words, he induced tears in anyone who happened to be near by. He could just as easily prompt gales of laughter. As a result, people were instinctively drawn to him and crowded around him.

Whenever anyone heard him begin to speak, they would prick their ears to hear what he had to say.

The goshawk screeched and leapt to Yakinahiko's arm — he wore a deerskin glove.

'Ketamaru, stay.'

Ketamaru could tell that his master was interested in the reed boat, so he was ready to fly to it. Just as Yakinahiko stretched out his other hand to calm the raptor, Ketamaru grazed it with his sharp talons, opening a gash on the palm. Blood spurted from the wound. Startled, Unashi raced to bind a white cloth around it. Yakinahiko clucked softly, mystified by what had happened. A goshawk is easy to train and always eager to obey its master. Why today had the bird put up a challenge?

Unashi stared nervously at the bandage he had wrapped around his master's hand, now saturated with blood. From his expression, you would have thought he was at fault.

'That's quite a wound.'

'It will heal quickly.' Knowing that Unashi was concerned, Yakinahiko tried to make light of the injury.

'It has sunk.' The helmsman pointed into the waves. The reed boat had disappeared.

Yakinahiko shook his head sadly. 'I wonder why they

float the child away in a boat like that. Burial would be better. Do you suppose the child can find any rest at the bottom of the sea?'

'That is what the people in these parts believe. And they trust the babe will be given new life and be born once more. That will be what they are praying for.' Unashi spoke as if he believed it himself. But Yakinahiko was not so sure. 'I wonder. To be alive is what matters most. Doesn't everything end with death? It makes no sense to mourn in this way – to send the pitiful babe away on a reed boat all alone.'

He felt a pang. Among the many children women had borne him, had there been any pitiful stillborns? Yakinahiko closed his eyes and thought about it but he could not recall. The number of women he had taken to wife, the number of children they had had, was far, far more than he could ever count.

His encounter with the tiny death on the high seas, so unexpected, had left him feeling uneasy. Having been granted eternal life, he had seen more than enough of death; understandably, he wished to avoid it now. Death was something to despise: it tore loving partners apart, forcing one to journey to a distant land while the other sank into a pool of sorrow. Death perpetrated an outrageous atrocity.

Not that Yakinahiko was completely aloof from death. He was a hunter, after all. He set out on journeys with the sole purpose of killing animals. So, his attitude was contradictory. When Yakinahiko hunted with Ketamaru, they caught small birds, like thrushes and larks, as well as pheasants and rabbits. As long as there was game, he would hunt it.

And the target of Yakinahiko's hunt was not always animals. He also pursued women. He sought virgins, or women at their peak – any woman for that matter, as long as she was a beauty. Once he caught wind of a beautiful woman, he would seek her out, no matter how far the quest might take him, and begin his seduction until he had won her from her father, her husband, her brothers. And, as though to atone for the lives of the animals he hunted, he granted the woman a child.

How many lives had he granted? In order to battle against the death he despised, he had had to continue bestowing life. That had become Yakinahiko's mission. And since it fell to the woman to raise the child, all Yakinahiko did was beget it, and then he was off, without a backward glance. He was always travelling, almost never to visit the same place twice. But this island chain was different.

'I wonder if Masago-hime is well.' Unashi said worriedly, as he gazed out over the waters ahead. He was close in age to the island princess and adored her as he would an older sister.

'I wonder,' Yakinahiko responded cheerfully. 'She's probably still swimming, even with that big belly.' He gazed into the blue sky. There wasn't a cloud in sight. For him to confront yet another unfamiliar sea voyage indicated the depth of his longing for Masago.

She was more beautiful than any other woman. Just twenty years old, her large black eyes were bewitching, her brows dark and thick, and her body enchanting. She stood almost as tall as Yakinahiko's chin, and her chest and hips were ample. When her skin – brown and supple – pressed against Yakinahiko's hard, sinewy body, he felt that she had been made just for him. Masago loved to run, swim, dive – she was always in motion. For Yakinahiko, who until then had known only delicate little Yamato women, hers was a special charm, impossible to resist.

And yet Yakinahiko was not able to stay long in any one place. If he did, it would become obvious that while others aged he did not. Finally he had decided to return to Yamato to resume the hunting he loved. When he had told Masago of his intention, she had cried and clung to him, pleading with him to stay at her side until at least she had delivered the baby.

Gathered up
From the bottom of the vast sea,
That shell becomes a bracelet,
Encircling your arm.
It accompanies you wherever you go.

This was the poem Masago had made when she had presented Yakinahiko with the armlet made of wide-mouth conch. For her Yakinahiko had recited:

> *'Brighter than any jewel,*
> *More beautiful than any gem,*
> *Of all the women I have loved,*
> *I love her best.*
> *Lady Masago.*
> *This love,*
> *Like a jewel,*
> *Sparkles in my heart.'*

And then he had taken the necklace that had never left his skin and placed it around Masago's neck, promising that he would return to her by the time she was to deliver her babe.

'I suppose she's had her baby by now,' Unashi mused.

'I wonder. I had hoped she would wait until I returned.'

Yakinahiko laughed as he said this. This time – and this was the only time – he longed to take this new life, his child, in his arms. The birth of a new life created by himself and his beloved Masago gave him great joy.

Unashi fought back shyness to say, 'I am sure that Masago-hime wanted to wait for her lord's return before delivering the child.'

2

The winds had been favourable and in no time at all the waves had calmed. Evening had fallen. By the following day they would be in Amaromi. Yakinahiko decided to entertain the sailors. Aboard ship, the fare was simple – whatever fish they had caught and sun-baked rice. But Yakinahiko pulled a large cask of *sake* out from his personal belongings, and Unashi offered it to the twenty or so sailors and the helmsman, who had gathered around him. 'Please, everyone, drink!'

Borne by a strong tail wind, the ship headed straight on course. The sky was clear and the glittering stars were reflected in the sea. At ease with the fine weather, the sailors bent happily over their wooden cups, their faces wreathed in smiles.

'Who has a story to tell about these islands?' The sailors exchanged glances with one another as Yakinahiko looked out over the seas. 'I'm always entertained by stories about places or things I've never seen.'

A middle-aged man with a beard broke the silence.

'Yakinahiko-sama, there are many islands in these seas. There was a time when I thought they were all like people – each with its own personality.'

'Interesting – give me an example.'

'Many islands almost bump against one another throughout these seas. One island will be home to poisonous snakes but the next island may not. That's often the case. Or on one island the people will be warm and friendly and on the neighbouring island they'll be quarrelsome. With only a short boat-ride between the two, they are as different as can be. That's why I feel each of the islands has a special character, just as people have their own personalities.'

'Are the women on the islands different as well?'

The sailors laughed. One short fellow stood up, a droll look on his face. 'Of course they are! The women on Ishiki-shima – a small island to the west – are known for being beautiful and working hard. They say that any man who takes an Ishiki woman to wife is fortunate indeed. But the women on the island next to it – Kokurika – are known to be plain. They're short and dark-skinned, and have screechy voices. And they make their husbands do whatever they say. A man who takes a Kokurika woman to wife is laughed at far and wide.'

'You know this from experience!' someone joked.

The sailor scratched his head, embarrassed. 'Well, yes, my wife is from Kokurika. But she has her charms.'

'You're smitten!'

All the men roared with laughter.

'And Amaromi?' Yakinahiko asked.

One of the young sailors sitting on the reed mat at his feet answered, 'You can't talk about Amaromi without mentioning Masago-hime. There's not another woman anywhere as beautiful as she. Compared to her the rest are just small fish.'

The other sailors sighed audibly in agreement. It seemed no one aboard ship knew that Masago was Yakinahiko's wife.

'Truly, she is the most beautiful woman in the world. We sail far and wide and I've never seen another as beautiful as she.'

Unashi filled everyone's cup again from the *sake* cask.

'Yakinahiko-sama,' a voice called from the dark, 'I wonder if you've ever heard of Umihebi Island, the Island of Sea Snakes?'

Yakinahiko swallowed his drink and shook his head. 'Where is it?'

The man who had spoken inched closer to the torch-light. Dressed in rags, he had white hair and a white beard – he was much older than one would expect a sailor to be. The other men, now fired up from their discussion of young women, looked at him with a touch of disgust. 'It's to the eastern edge of the chain. No more than a little speck.'

If it was on the eastern edge, it would be where the sun rose. Yakinahiko's interest quickened. He turned to the old man, and asked, 'Why is it known as the Island of Sea Snakes?'

'A sacred sea snake called *naganawa-sama* lives in the waters off the island. In spring, all the women on the island gather together and collect as many as they can catch alive and put them in a large storehouse. After the *naganawa-sama* have dried out, they eat them. I've heard they use the eggs to make a nutritious broth. It's said to be delicious, but I've never tasted it. I've heard that only a few people are permitted to enjoy it – those who are required to live long lives.'

'What of the island?' Yakinahiko, eager to learn more, urged the man to continue.

Perhaps because he sensed that he had captured Yakinahiko's curiosity, the old man opened his mouth in a wide, toothless grin. 'That island boasts a beauty. Now, Masago-hime is a beautiful woman, to be sure, but this woman is exceptionally lovely. If it's a fair-skinned beauty you seek, she's the fairest in all the islands. She's tall

and supple, a fine singer and dancer, and her face is so
exquisite that once you see her you can't look away. She's
no maiden, but I've heard that you need only meet her
once to fall so madly in love you might swear you had
been bewitched.'

A warm night breeze blew gently over the men. They
listened silently. One among them closed his eyes as
though he were trying to imagine the kind of woman
she might be.

'Her age?' another asked.

'Perhaps half mine,' the old man responded, causing
a large number of his fellows to sigh with relief.

'What is her name?' Yakinahiko asked.

'Kamikuu-sama, the great Oracle.'

As soon as they heard she was an oracle, a priestess,
most of the men shook their heads, crestfallen. But
Yakinahiko was undaunted. He didn't care if she were a
princess or a priestess. A woman was a woman. And the
name 'Kamikuu' was carved upon his heart.

'She must be untouchable, if she is a priestess,' one
of the younger men said drunkenly.

'Not Kamikuu-sama. She's a life-giver. She must make
as many babies as she can — the more men she has the
better. Some man will wink at her and, if all goes well,
she'll bring him into her bedroom. But it's essential that

the man takes her fancy. She won't have just anyone. And I hear she has only men who are easy on the eye – like Yakinahiko-sama here.'

The sailors turned in unison to look at him. One of the younger men shouted, 'The rest of us don't stand a chance, then. Not to mention the young Masago-sama who won't even look in our direction!'

The rest burst out laughing, ending their talk of women. They resumed drinking.

'Yakinahiko-sama?' Unashi murmured quietly, at his master's side. Yakinahiko, seated, looked up at him. 'What the man was saying – I don't understand. How could he possibly compare Masago-hime to a middle-aged woman on a pitiful island like that? '

'Oh, don't be too hard on him. This is a big world we live in. And wherever you go you'll find beautiful women, each with her own charms. You can't compare one to another. Besides, you never know. A beautiful woman might be as stiff as a puppet in the bedroom while an ugly one gives her man pleasure. Hard to say who'd be the winner.' Yakinahiko had parried the challenge from his young attendant.

'But, Yakinahiko-sama, aren't you devoted to Masago-hime? After all, you've never returned to any of your other wives, so I assumed she must be a very special woman.'

Unashi drilled home the truth, leaving Yakinahiko momentarily without a retort.

'I don't love Masago simply because of her beauty. I am devoted to her from the bottom of my heart. I love her body and soul. I love her beautiful spirit – the way she longs for me so deeply she would give her life for me. I wonder if any other woman would die for my sake.'

Unashi's youthful face darkened.

'Unashi, if there's something you want to say to me, please do so.'

'It's nothing. If you'll excuse me, I'll give Ketamaru his meal.' Unashi bowed and went below deck.

Suddenly Yakinahiko was assailed by an unspeakable fear. He gazed into the night sky at the stars glittering brightly. The ship slipped quietly over the waves. Nothing was amiss.

'Yakinahiko-sama, thank you for treating us to your delicious *sake*.' The helmsman had stepped up beside him.

'Not at all. It is I who should thank you. You let us board your ship without so much as a moment's notice.'

'Say nothing of it!' The helmsman bowed. 'It is an honour to have a nobleman such as yourself with us. A while back you asked us to entertain you with our stories. Well, I was just reminded of something. If you will allow me, I'd like to tell it.'

The helmsman set aside his wooden *sake* cup as he prepared to launch into his tale. The other sailors gathered around, eager to hear. 'It was about half a year ago. I let a sparrow wasp aboard ship,' he began, as Unashi reappeared.

'A wasp, you say?' Unashi asked.

'That's right. It was large and yellow with black stripes. The sailor who saw it perched on the water barrel was startled and tried to kill it. The wasp took off over the waves. But then it returned, and when the sailors saw it, they all tried to kill it. When I heard the commotion, I came over to investigate. It looked as though the wasp was reluctant to leave the ship. It was as if it had chosen to stay because it had somewhere to go. So, I came up with a test. "If you promise not to sting anyone, you can ride with us. Fly in a circle if you agree," I said to it. Sure enough, it flew in a circle. It was the strangest thing. Surprised us all! So, we let it stay with us and treated it as if it was our guardian deity.'

'What became of the wasp?'

'Well, it did what it could to stay out of our way and took passage on the ship. Mostly it stayed below and lived off the insects there. Now and then it would fly over to the water barrel and sip the water that had splashed along the edge.'

'Did it pay for passage?' a man interjected, and everyone laughed.

'On that journey we didn't stop at Amaromi but went straight on to Nahariha Island. As soon as we reached Nahariha, the wasp left the ship and, as if to offer its gratitude, flew around us a number of times in a circle.'

'That is unusual,' Yakinahiko murmured.

The helmsman nodded. 'And that's not all. I heard that a man died from a wasp's sting on Umihebi Island, the island the old man was telling you about, the one with the great Oracle. And that was just after the wasp left our ship.'

'Surely that's just a coincidence.' Yakinahiko looked doubtful.

The helmsman shook his head. 'It wasn't a coincidence, Yakinahiko-sama, because they've never had wasps on that island. Just like you heard a little while ago. There are islands with poisonous snakes and islands without them. Each island has its own character. And on Umihebi Island they've never had wasps. So the only possible explanation is that the wasp that took passage on my ship was the one they found on the island.'

'Are you suggesting the wasp was going to Umihebi Island when it boarded your ship?'

The helmsman cocked his head to the side and sighed.

'I don't know. All I can say is that the wasp took my ship from Yamato.'

'They say a wasp can fly close to twenty-five leagues a day,' said the old sailor who had earlier spoken of Umihebi Island. 'That's close to seventy-five miles! So, I suppose it could have flown from Nahariha to Umihebi.'

Yakinahiko stared out over the waves, trying to imagine a wasp's flight.

At last the moon began to sink in the west and the drinking party came to an end. Yakinahiko was in a fine mood, having enjoyed cup after cup of *sake*. Unashi took him by the hand and led him staggering to the hold beneath the stern where he put him into the bed he'd prepared. Next Unashi pulled a black cloth over Ketamaru's cage.

'Yakinahiko-sama, does the wound on your hand hurt?' Unashi asked his master with concern.

Yakinahiko stared at the white bandage encircling it. The bleeding had stopped. By tomorrow the mark would have disappeared. Immortal as he was, Yakinahiko bled on occasion but wounds soon healed and left no scar.

'It's much better.' Yakinahiko pulled his hand behind his back, not wishing Unashi to inquire any further. 'More than that, though, Unashi, we should be thinking of Amaromi. We will be there by tomorrow, the winds having been so favourable.'

'That's true.'

Unashi was not very talkative, Yakinahiko thought. He recalled that while they were drinking with the sailors, he had seemed a little down. 'Unashi, are you keeping something from me?'

Unashi shook his head stubbornly. 'No. Yakinahiko-sama, you are imagining things.'

Yakinahiko looked hard at Unashi's crescent-shaped eyes. He had chosen Unashi to be his attendant when the latter was just a boy of twelve. That was seven years ago, and now Unashi had grown so tall he had nearly caught up with his master. His shoulders were broad and his arms and legs muscular. His voice had deepened as well. In all respects he was very nearly a full-grown adult man. Had he noticed that, over the last seven years, Yakinahiko had not changed at all?

Yakinahiko knew that the day was fast approaching when he would have to leave Unashi, before Unashi became suspicious. His chest tightened with sorrow. He had outlived wives, children, attendants, his birds – all had died before him, and then others had been born to take their place. He was the only one to continue living. Again and again he had brought children into the world, but how futile it seemed. Seized suddenly with apprehension about his body, he stared at his fingers under the light from the candles.

'What's the matter?'

'Unashi, do I look old to you?'

'Not at all, Yakinahiko-sama. You look as young as the day I met you. You haven't changed a bit. Your eyesight is sharp, your chest is broad and strong and, far from losing courage, you have grown even more spirited. You are a man among men. An extraordinary man.'

Unashi spoke from his heart, then dropped his gaze awkwardly. His sensitive soul was part of his charm.

3

The following day the weather was clear and beautiful as Amaromi came into view, nestled beneath a luxuriant green canopy of oaks. The ship, now at the end of its voyage, waited for high tide before sailing into the harbour. The jetty that stretched from the wide beach to the shoals had been fashioned from piles of white limestone rocks. The blue sky, the water so clear you could see the white sands at the bottom of the sea, the green-canopied island, the white jetty. Surely Masago had come down to meet his ship. Yakinahiko searched the shore for sight of her. But she was nowhere to be seen. Instead, he noticed a man wearing a short white garment, his legs exposed, standing with a dazed expression.

Why did the little reed boat they had seen mid-journey flash through Yakinahiko's mind? He was seized with a terrible premonition. Not waiting for the ship to reach its moorings, he leapt from the deck to the jetty, the helmsman and the sailors watching from the gunwale. When they saw the man in white step out to meet him, their faces uniformly stiffened. The short white robe was the garment of mourning.

'Welcome back, Yakinahiko-sama.'

The man awaiting him at the jetty was Masago's father, the chief of Amaromi Island. As soon as Yakinahiko drew closer and saw that his face was twisted with sorrow, he knew disaster was imminent. 'What has happened?'

'I am sorry for the shock this will bring you, but Masago died seven days ago.'

Yakinahiko froze, unable to comprehend what he had heard.

Unashi gave a loud wail. 'That cannot be true!'

The chief was unable to answer.

'Was the birth difficult?' Yakinahiko asked. 'Was that it?'

The chief slowly shook his head. 'No, she delivered the child safely. My wife is looking after the baby now.'

'So how did she die? Was an illness going round?'

'I don't know.' The chief's face darkened. 'It was so sudden. She didn't even seem to be sick. One day she spoke of feeling cold water splash her cheek, and then she was gone.'

'Cold water?'

It was so mysterious, and Yakinahiko was lost in confusion.

'Masago delivered the baby three weeks ago. It was an easy birth and she recovered quickly afterwards. She was so looking forward to your return, Yakinahiko-sama, knowing you would soon be back. And then, just seven days ago, while she was nursing the baby, she complained of a great pain. She fell where she was and said, "A splash of water . . . so cold," and she was gone. Everything happened so quickly, I feel as if I'm in a dream. The whole village is in shock. We are all at a loss.'

'For a young woman as robust as she to die so suddenly is sad beyond measure. How fleeting is this world of ours.' Yakinahiko was overwhelmed with sorrow.

Unashi, with tears streaming down his cheeks, whispered, 'Yakinahiko-sama, please tell me why this is happening.'

'What do you mean, Unashi?'

Unashi bit his lip, as if he was afraid to explain himself. Yakinahiko urged him to speak his mind, but just then the chief began again.

'Yakinahiko-sama, would you like to see the baby?'

Yakinahiko walked behind the chief as he led them up a path paved with broken white shells. In the stilted house at the top of the hill, Masago's mother, also dressed in white mourning clothes, waited, the baby cradled in her arms. 'The keepsake Masago left behind.'

Crying as she spoke, the mother handed the baby to Yakinahiko.

How many thousands of children had he fathered? Rather, how many millions? Yakinahiko asked himself, as he held the tiny infant in his arms. But even as he peered into the baby's face, he did not feel any particular tug at his heart. At least the baby had not been the cause of its mother's death . . . at least she had had that good fortune.

'Have you named her?'

'Masago named her Sango for the coral.'

Sango-hime – princess of coral. It was not a propitious name, for now the white bones of the coral would for ever be associated with Masago's death. Yakinahiko gazed down at the baby asleep in his arms. He didn't need this child, he thought. He would rather have Masago returned to him. Without warning, tears fell from his eyes.

When the chief saw this, he touched Yakinahiko's hand. 'Would you like to see Masago?'

'See her?'

'She's dead, of course, cold, but if you would go to see her, it will make her happy in the next world.'

Yakinahiko could hear a voice inside him telling him not to go. But they had been separated for nearly a year and all that time he had loved her dearly. Stronger than the feeling not to go was the desire to see her face just one more time.

With the chief as his guide, Yakinahiko went to the burial ground on the northern end of the island. On Amaromi, the dead were placed in caves dug out of the cliffs that faced the sea. Unashi followed a few feet behind his master, with Ketamaru on his left arm, perched on the falconer's glove.

'As is the custom of our island, the dead are laid out in the open, exposed to the elements, until the flesh disappears. After years have passed, we draw water from the sea and wash the bones. When that happens, the spirit is finally released into the heavens, and they say that that is when the spirit departs for the land of the gods on the other side of the sea.'

After the chief had scrambled over crags and through thickets of hardy pemphis shrubs, he began to climb a wall of black rock, with Yakinahiko and Unashi behind him. Midway up it, any number of large rectangular caves had been carved out by the waves. When the chief beckoned the other two towards one, they noticed a strong odour. Masago's body had begun to decay. Yakinahiko faltered. The chief, seemingly unaware of his hesitation, continued to beckon him forward. Yakinahiko was her husband: of course he would want to see her.

'Masago's in here.'

There was a brand new coffin towards the opening of the cave. The chief had said the bodies were exposed to the elements so the coffin had no lid. He urged Yakinahiko to stand beside the coffin and look into it. Overcome by the stench, he covered his nose with his left hand and peered in reluctantly.

There could be no doubt that the body inside was Masago's. Upon her beautiful brow they had set a square amulet made of shell to ward off evil. Her eyes were closed. The flesh on her face had begun to sag, and she did not look like her former self. The skin on her hands, crossed over her breast, had turned black and was beginning to fester.

'Masago,' Yakinahiko called. Yet it was impossible to think of the corpse in the coffin as his Masago, the woman who had once been so beautiful that he had felt reluctant even to draw close to her. The thought of embracing the thing lying before him was so horrifying it made him tremble. He was afraid – and fear brought with it memories of a distant past.

He had once been the male deity Izanaki, and his wife, Izanami, had died. His longing to see her again was more than he could bear so he had pursued her into the Realm of the Dead. She had warned him, 'Do not look at me,' but eventually he had peered in at her to find she had turned into a rotting corpse. She might once have been his wife but now she was something entirely different.

And so it was here. The body laid out in the coffin had once been a beautiful woman, his wife, but not any more. Now she was a stinking, rotting corpse. Why, Yakinahiko wondered, was he, who had seen so much of death, still repulsed when confronted with it?

'Yakinahiko-sama, are you all right?'

He could hear Ketamaru's wings flapping. Unashi, ever stalwart, rushed up to steady him, afraid he was about to collapse. Yakinahiko looked one more time at his wife's oozing flesh. He couldn't turn and run with the chief standing in front of him. Then he saw that the jade necklace he had given his wife had slipped to the ground. Yakinahiko picked it up and said to the chief, 'This once hung around her neck, but it seems the cord's been cut.'

'It must have happened while we were carrying her up here.'

To Yakinahiko, it looked more as if someone had sliced into it – a bad omen. 'Let us give it to Masago's little Sango as a memento.'

When you're dead, there's nothing left so such things should stay with the living, not go with the dead. He had intended to divide the string of jewels, but when he remembered how Masago's face had lit up when he had given it to her, he was beset with sorrow.

'How happy Masago would be to hear you say such a thing.'

'And in exchange I will leave this with Masago. It is something I have valued more than my life.'

Yakinahiko slipped off the shell armlet and placed it on Masago's breast. It was the armlet she had made for him, wishing that she might, like the armlet, accompany him on his journey. But returning it to her now signified Yakinahiko's desire to be free of her corpse.

While the chief stared at his daughter, seemingly loath to leave her side, Yakinahiko left the cave and virtually flew down the side of the cliff. The chief most likely attributed his haste to grief. But it was fear. Death was defiling. Having seen something so defiled, Yakinahiko had to purify himself. When he had gone to see Izanami in the Realm of the Dead, he had been terrified by what he had seen and had fled through the darkness to the opening of the cave. That time he had been pursued. When he'd looked back he had seen a horde of warriors and women who looked like demons. But surely it had been his own fear that had chased him.

'Yakinahiko-sama, your grief must be unbearable.'

The chief had followed him and had spoken with the

deepest sympathy as he had gazed into Yakinahiko's blanched face. Yakinahiko nodded without a word. All he could think about was purifying himself. 'Is there a fresh spring near by?' he asked.

'You will find one by the cave where we bury the dead. Its waters always flow fresh.'

Guided by the chief, Yakinahiko reached it. He pulled off the white bandage and washed both of his hands. He rinsed his eyes, removed his white garments and, completely naked, ordered Unashi to throw water over him.

'But I have no bucket.'

'Then use your hands.'

Unashi tethered Ketamaru to a tangled banyan branch and began scooping water from the spring with his hands. He splashed it over every inch of Yakinahiko's firm flesh. Yakinahiko closed his eyes and remembered. He had bathed in the waters of the river on the Plain of Awaki-ga-hara in Himuka. When he came back to himself he found that he was weeping.

'What is it?' Unashi asked worriedly, as he circled his master, uncertain what to do.

Yakinahiko collapsed to his knees and continued to weep. He remembered the tiny reed boat. The first child that he, Izanaki, had produced after coupling with his wife Izanami, had had no bones: they had put it into a reed boat and set it adrift on the seas. Now humans imitated what the gods had done. Why then, Yakinahiko wondered, did he find it so ill-omened when he saw the practice, having become a human himself? What had gone wrong? Who had done this to him?

The sun was sinking in the west. Unashi was still at his side, kneeling. They were both in tears. The chief had disappeared.

'Where is the chief?'

'He withdrew out of respect for your grief. '

'That's for the best,' Yakinahiko muttered, as he dressed. He noticed that Unashi was staring in surprise at his left hand. He should have had a gash where Ketamaru had clawed him, but the wound had healed without a scar. Yakinahiko hurriedly covered his right hand, but Unashi prostrated himself at his feet.

'Yakinahiko-sama, what manner of man are you?'

'Do you think I am not of this world?'

Still face down on the ground, Unashi replied, 'I do not know. All I know is that I have never in my life met a man like you. You amaze me. Surely you are someone − some*thing* − that exceeds human understanding.'

'Are you afraid of me? Am I a monster?'

For a few minutes Unashi did not answer. Then he said, 'No. I'm not afraid of you. It's just that . . .'

'What?'

'When I think you're not a man like me, it makes me sad. And someone as extraordinary as you are cannot possibly be human.'

'Unashi, when you saw Masago's corpse, how did you feel?'

Unashi answered, without looking up, 'It was so sad to think that someone as beautiful as Masago-hime would end up rotting away, no better than an animal. But it'll be the same for me when I die. That's just the way it is, and we humans can't escape our fate. But it makes living all the more precious.'

So that was it. For humans, death was inescapable. Yakinahiko had not thought of it like that before. But what about Izanami? She was a god. What was death to her? He had not thought about her for so long.

He could feel the tide retreating. The smell of the sea was now strong. Even inside the cave on the cliff, the blowing of the sea winds had been strong. Perhaps the winds would carry Masago's festering smell far away. Yakinahiko's mood began to lighten. He asked Unashi, 'What is worrying you? Any number of times you have seemed about to ask me something and then you lose your tongue. Ask – please.'

Unashi raised his youthful, sunburnt face and finally

looked Yakinahiko in the eye. 'Very well. You have many wives. I've watched you select the most beautiful woman in any region we've visited and make her your wife. I've watched you call out to them, as if you were on a mission. Eventually I realised that marrying women *is* your mission, your job. But recently I've noticed a disturbing trend.'

'What's that?'

Yakinahiko noticed how frightened Unashi looked. Had the boy grasped that he never aged? Or that his wounds healed immediately? To come upon an immortal could only be unnerving for a human, whose body changed constantly. Yakinahiko was prepared to explain, but Unashi's answer caught him off guard.

'Of the women who bear your children, most die suddenly. And because you never travel to the same place twice, you haven't noticed. But I've heard rumours time and again. There was Kuro-sama of Awa and Kariha-sama in Mozuno, and many, many more. And I have heard that all of them died as soon as they gave birth to one of your children. Why is that?'

Taken by surprise, Yakinahiko was unable to answer straight away. And when he did, all he could say was, 'That is the first I've heard of it. Kuro and Kariha are both dead?'

'Yes. It was very sad – they died so suddenly. That's why I was beside myself with worry over whether Masago-hime was faring well or not.'

'Is that so? I thought you were worried about Masago because you had special feelings for her. She was a very lovely woman.'

'She was.' Unashi nodded. 'I was worried but I couldn't believe Masago-sama would meet a similar fate. After all, she lived so far from Yamato. But death has come here as well, even for her. It is chasing you, Yakinahiko-sama. And I have a thought that is almost too terrifying to mention.'

'What's that, Unashi?'

The evening sun had nearly set. A sliver glimmered over the sea to the west – the colour of madder berries. Yakinahiko thought that it would be best to make for the village before the curtain of night fell, but for some reason he could not move.

Unashi hesitated, then asked, 'Yakinahiko-sama, have you incurred someone's hatred?'

'Perhaps.' Yakinahiko sat down on a large white rock and sighed. He thought of the words he and Izanami had exchanged before they parted.

'My beloved Izanaki, your behaviour is reprehensible. You have trapped me in this place, and now you say you wish a divorce. From this day forward, therefore, I will take the lives of one thousand people each day in your land of the living.'

To this Izanaki had responded: 'My beloved Izanami, you may do as you say, but I shall build fifteen hundred birthing huts and will daily see that fifteen hundred new lives are born.'

When Izanaki had finally escaped from Izanami, he had purified his body, and then had given birth to a number of gods, including Amaterasu, the radiant Sun Goddess. Then, upon assuming human form, he had taken the name Yakinahiko and had travelled throughout Yamato impregnating women. If Izanami had caused the deaths of those he had taken to wife, then truly death was the victor. He did not want another wife to lose her life.

Yakinahiko was overcome by sorrow.

'Unashi, my fate is irrevocable and I have no choice but to accept it. It is my fate to search out women, get them with child, then watch them die. If I love the woman, the pain I feel at her death is all the greater, so I must not fall in love. But even so, it is, as you say, my mission to give them children.'

'May I ask why? I've grown up since I entered your service so, for me, you are like a parent. No, you are more like a god to me. I met you when I was only twelve, and from that time on I've been so awed by your magnificent spirit that all I've ever wanted was to be at your side. I want to understand your pain and sorrow – I want to share everything with you. I will accept the truth, no matter how cruel, no matter if it is so mysterious no mere mortal could comprehend it.'

Unashi was trembling as he spoke, swaying with fear. At that moment the heavens rolled with thunder and rain began to fall. Surely it was dripping into Masago's coffin, washing the flesh from her bones. Soaked though he was, Yakinahiko stood gazing up at the cave. Now all he could see was a dark opening carved into the side of the cliff.

'Please, tell me,' Unashi shouted, to be heard over the thunder.

'Very well. I will. But you must not be frightened.'

'I promise.' Unashi gritted his teeth.

4

After the downpour, everything was refreshed and the sky was clear and serene, as if it had been scrubbed clean. A yellow moon had risen in the night sky, glittering brightly. Yakinahiko had told Unashi that he was the god Izanaki and about the discord with his wife, Izanami. Now he sat on a rock and stared at the moon, feeling depleted. Unashi lay on the sand, unmoving. Yakinahiko imagined that he had been shocked when he had heard Izanami's parting words to him.

Finally, Unashi lifted his tear-stained face. 'Yakinahiko-sama, is Izanami-sama strangling the life out of any woman who becomes your wife?'

'I don't know.'

'But if she is, you cannot stop her.'

'That's right.'

Yakinahiko looked over his shoulder at the cave in the cliff. He could just make out, in the moonlight, the tip of Masago's white coffin. The woman he loved was now rotting inside that cave. The loneliness made him so sad he felt as if his entire body were being torn asunder. When your companion dies, all the time you would have shared together dies as well. It was lonely for the departed, but far more so for the one left behind. What had become of his sympathy when Izanami had died when he was a god? Yakinahiko had long been indifferent towards the dead because he was immortal, and the defilement of death terrified him. But now, when he thought it over, he wondered if perhaps the opposite were true. Perhaps he had desired immortality because he was terrified of death's defilement. At any rate, to live without end meant that he could never truly love a woman or live his life with Unashi.

'Neither Izanami nor I will ever be free of our parting words.' Yakinahiko stood up. He threw his wet clothes down and started to run, naked, over the rocks, hoping he might just disappear for ever from the face of the earth. He clambered over the ragged crags and when he reached the top of the cliff, he dove into the sea, some twenty or thirty feet below. But he failed to strike his head on a rock and succeeded merely in scooping up a handful of sand from the ocean floor. His mouth filled with the salty water, as his body bobbed to the surface. He did not try to move but his body floated. He could not die. It was impossible.

'Yakinahiko-sama! Yakinahiko-sama!' Unashi was scrambling over the rocks, calling his name. 'What are you doing?'

Yakinahiko waved and began to swim to him. 'Nothing's the matter,' he replied, as he strode out of the ocean. Cold drops of water ran from his body as he scaled the crags.

Unashi ran up to him, out of breath. 'All of a sudden you just leapt into the ocean – you gave me quite a scare.'

'Did you see, Unashi? No matter what I do, I cannot die. A while ago I slipped from a precipice and split my head open. But the next morning I was back to normal. I've been tangled up in wars and had an arrow through my chest. That time I died momentarily. The next day the holes in my body had filled in and I had returned to life.'

'So, Yakinahiko-sama, when I grow old, even when I die, you'll still be just as you are now?'

'Yes. Does that terrify you?'

Unashi shook his head. 'No. I think it's pitiful. People say they want to live for ever but someone who's immortal must be very lonely. I wouldn't be able to stand it.'

It was like Unashi to be so perceptive. Yakinahiko loved him all the more. He had never meant to cause his young attendant such distress.

'Yakinahiko-sama, what do you want to do? I will do whatever I can to help you, even give my life for yours. Please, tell me what you would have me do.'

'I want to die. If I don't die, Izanami's rancour will never end. My wives will continue dying for all eternity. Please, could you kill me?' Yakinahiko asked.

Unashi began to cry. 'I understand. I couldn't bear to be parted from you, but if that is what you really want, I will try. You must tell me how to end your life. If you know what I should do, please tell me and I will do it!'

Yakinahiko showed Unashi his left hand. 'Look at my hand. Yesterday Ketamaru left a deep gash with his talons and today there is no trace of the wound. You can stab me, even slice me to pieces, and tomorrow I'll be whole again.'

'But you said you wanted me to end your life.' The moon shone in Unashi's eyes, a clear, sharp light.

'That's right,' Yakinahiko responded, and cradled the boy's head in his arms. 'But it's not possible.'

'Yakinahiko-sama, have you ever killed anyone?'

Yakinahiko shook his head. 'Animals I kill day and night — too many ever to count — but never a person. When I was Izanaki I copulated with my female consort and created this island country. I made other gods. I made children. I had no business with death. All the more reason why I had to part with Izanami once she died and went to the Realm of the Dead.'

'Why don't you kill me and see if that makes a difference?'

Yakinahiko was shocked. 'Why would I kill you?'

'Because something might happen.' Unashi's answer was not convincing. 'I think there's value in trying.'

'But there's no point in your dying, Unashi.'

'From what you've told me, Izanami is responsible for death and Izanaki for life. The roles are very clearly drawn. If you did something that was the complete opposite, don't you think it might make a difference?'

'Why don't you kill me and I'll kill you? Let's die together and see what happens. Death – should we both succeed – would be a happy outcome.'

Before he had finished speaking Yakinahiko began to tremble at the thought of what he had proposed. The odds were high that Unashi would die but that he himself would revive.

'I'm ready. I will gladly give my life for you. And if Masago-hime knew that her death was the result of her association with you, I'm sure she would feel content. That's what love is. You, too – you loved Masago-hime body and soul. That was what you told me yesterday.'

Unashi urged Yakinahiko on with such adult assurance

it was difficult to believe he was just nineteen. Surely if he killed the man he admired and if in turn he were killed by that man, he would die peacefully. Yakinahiko unsheathed the long sword at his hip. Unashi was trembling as he pulled out his own blade. Ketamaru, waiting in the shade of the banyan, sensed that something was afoot and gave a piercing cry.

'Yakinahiko-sama, thank you for everything you've done for me.' As Unashi delivered his final words, a dark cloud floated across the moon.

'If we are successful, we will meet again in the Realm of the Dead.'

After Yakinahiko had spoken his final words, he gave Unashi the signal. 'Strike!'

He sank his blade deep into Unashi's throat. At the same time, he felt the force of sharp steel thrust into his own. Before he could sense pain, his throat filled with blood.

How much time had passed, he did not know. Yakinahiko opened his eyes in the darkness. He could hear the sound of the sea and the wind roaring above him. He spat out the sand in his mouth and leapt to his feet. His head hurt and he struggled to come to his senses. He remembered nothing.

Beside him a man dressed in white lay on the ground with his throat split open. His body was regal and his hair, pulled atop his head in two bunches, was ornamented with jewels. The blood from his wound had soaked into the sand, turning the ground around him black.

'Unashi, you died, didn't you?'

The memory of their murder pact rushed through him like a torrent. Yakinahiko hurried to Unashi's side and took him in his arms. Despair infused him as he realised that he alone had continued living. Then he jumped to his feet in shock. The man lying before him was not Unashi. It was himself — Yakinahiko. At least, it was Yakinahiko's body, lifeless, surrounded by blood. But who was he? Yakinahiko felt his throat. There was no wound. He looked at his hands. They were the hands of a young man, the knuckles still smooth and not pronounced. Was it possible that he was Unashi? If he was Unashi, he should have two moles on his left arm. He frantically tore his clothes off and carefully examined his arm in the moonlight. And there he found the moles. When they had struck each other, had his body expired while Unashi's lived on? Unashi's spirit must have died so that his own had inhabited Unashi's body. Overwhelmed by the knowledge that he had killed Unashi, Yakinahiko collapsed in tears.

'I have no idea what tomorrow will bring.'

Would Yakinahiko's body return to life, as it always had in the past? Or had Unashi's body now become immortal? Yakinahiko decided to put it to a test. He picked up the sword he had dropped earlier and sliced Unashi's palm with the tip. The pain was excruciating and blood spurted from the wound. He watched in silence. He wondered if the wound would be gone by morning. Meanwhile, the blood oozed without stopping.

Day broke. At some point he must have fallen asleep, the blood still flowing from his palm. Ketamaru's piercing cries awoke him. He walked over to Yakinahiko's body, the body that until recently had been his own. Nothing had changed. It was still dead. Unashi's wound, conversely, still bled.

Yakinahiko was unable to find the words to express his feelings. He had assumed the youthful body of a nineteen-year-old man. A mortal man. At last he was mortal! He had lost his steadfast retainer, but in return, he had become a real human man. Destroying Unashi's youthful spirit had allowed him to steal into a boy's young body. But his punishment for slaughtering a human was to lose his god status. He had, after all, been the God of Birth.

'From now I shall live as Unashi.'

So resolved, he began to feel throughout his entire being the wondrousness of Unashi's youth – the suppleness of his skin, the flexibility of his muscles. 'Well, then. Your master is dead. You can go wherever you please.' Unashi untied the cords that bound Ketamaru and released him into the sky. Ketamaru gave a shrill cry and circled Yakinahiko's corpse. He soared away and seemed to have gone when suddenly he returned with a large snake clutched in his hook-like talons. Taking aim at Unashi, he dropped the snake. There were plenty of poisonous snakes on Amaromi. It seemed that Ketamaru, believing that Unashi had killed his master, was seeking revenge. Unashi sliced the snake in two with his sword and shouted, 'Ketamaru! Yakinahiko is dead. Go and tell your fellow birds.'

The goshawk cut circles in the air and screeched. The wound on Unashi's palm ached. When he looked at it, he realised that the snake had bitten him before it had died: one of its tiny fangs had lodged itself in the wound. He withdrew the fang, but the poison had entered his blood. His left arm began to swell and turn red. It felt heavy now. So heavy that he found himself unexpectedly falling to his knees. The goshawk flew off, seemingly satisfied. Unashi smiled bitterly at the irony. The bird had meant to take revenge on the man who had slain his master, but its revenge was played out on none other than Yakinahiko, now transformed into Unashi.

'Unashi-sama! Are you all right?'

The cry was full of alarm. When Unashi and Yakinahiko had not returned by morning, the island chief and his attendant had come to search for them. The chief froze when he saw Yakinahiko's body.

'How did Yakinahiko die?'

'He was overcome with grief and determined to take his own life. I tried to stop him, but his intent was too strong and he would not be deterred.'

Unashi developed a high fever and lost consciousness. He lingered in a near-death coma for more than two weeks. While he was ill, the village conducted Yakinahiko's funeral. His corpse was placed next to Masago-hime's, and the two lay side by side like a happy couple. When the years passed and their bodies disintegrated, surely their spirits would slip together across the seas to reside in the land of the gods.

5

Two months later, when Unashi had regained his strength and was able to venture out, he went to visit Yakinahiko and Masago's tomb. When he gazed upon Yakinahiko's corpse – which was actually his own – he was struck by the uncanniness of what he had experienced.

'Who are you, lying here before me, emitting this foul stench? Are you Izanaki? Or the outer shell of Yakinahiko? Or perhaps I have before me Unashi's heart. But no, his heart is within my own body. And that shows what a complete illusion the human body is. All that remains is the heart.'

Shells to ward off evil had been placed on the broad forehead of the body that had belonged to Yakinahiko, just as had been done with Masago's corpse. The eye sockets had collapsed and now lay exposed to the bright rays of the sun.

'But I'm sure it'll be the same for me when I die . . . We humans can't escape our fate. But it makes living all the more precious.'

The real Unashi had murmured these words after viewing Masago's corpse. For the first time in all his existence the new Unashi confronted the impermanence of the human body; its fragility made him cry out in dismay. How weak and foolish he had been – he who had despised the very sight of those festering bodies, Izanami's long ago, and now Masago's.

'I have before me the flesh that once housed Yakinahiko. I am setting off on a journey with Unashi's spirit, and I doubt I will see you again, old friend. It is best for you to scatter with the wind, to melt into the earth.'

Unashi placed Yakinahiko's long sword, bow and arrows in the coffin and walked out of the tomb. He was ready to leave Amaromi Island.

'Unashi-sama, where are you going?' The island chief, still dressed in his white mourning robe, asked, as Unashi was busy putting his things together for travel. On Amaromi Island the period of mourning continued until it was time to wash the bones. For two years those in mourning would continue to wear the ceremonial white robes.

Unashi, handsome in his white robes, stared at the chief's sunburnt face. 'Now that Yakinahiko-sama is dead

I see no reason to return to Yamato. I feel all the stronger about pushing further south, to islands not yet seen. As luck would have it, the helmsman I know is in port now, and I may ask him to take me on as a sailor.'

The island chief was shocked. 'Unashi-sama, there's no need for you to assume such a task – to become a sailor! You were Yakinahiko's trusted retainer. Wouldn't it be better for you to stay with us on Amaromi? As long as you are here you will not need to put yourself to such hard labour. We have young women aplenty on the island. I will find you a nice wife, and you can make your home with us.'

Then Masago's mother spoke up, her eyes spilling tears: 'To do the work of a sailor with your handicap! How hard it will be for you!'

Unashi had lost his left hand. That was the one the viper had bitten, and because it was believed the left hand was close to the heart, the island's chief had amputated it to save Unashi's life. All the islanders were overwhelmed with pity for the young man who had not only lost his master Yakinahiko – who had taken his own life – but also his hand.

But Unashi did not care whether he had his left hand or not. In fact, the missing limb reminded him that his body was now mortal. At last Yakinahiko – having assumed the form of Unashi – was able to experience a human body that did not revert to its original health following injury or illness but was growing older day by day. Yakinahiko had decided that he would continue to live in Unashi's body, until that body had come to the end of its natural life. Moreover, having suddenly transformed into Unashi, he was now eager to enjoy life as a nineteen-year-old.

The helmsman of the shellfish trawler well remembered Yakinahiko's young attendant. When Unashi asked to be taken on as a sailor, he immediately agreed. Using his teeth, Unashi was able to unknot the mooring line, hoist the sail and, with his one arm, ply the oar. All in all, he did such a fine job as a sailor that soon he aspired to become a helmsman.

When the ship carrying Unashi finally sailed into the harbour off Umihebi Island, more than a year had passed since Yakinahiko's death. The white cliffs of the island glinted under the light of a full moon, and to the left stretched a long strand of white beaches. Having decided to wait for the following morning before putting in to port, the sailors were lounging on the deck.

Unashi, however, was below deck, battling pain. From

time to time his missing left hand would throb so sharply it caused beads of sweat to form on his brow. He'd suffer agony one day and on the next the pain would be gone 'A wound never heals so long as your heart remembers the pain,' he remembered the old sailor telling him – the same old man who had told them about the priestess on Umihebi Island. When Unashi had been Yakinahiko, whatever pain he might suffer was short-lived. Now, tormented by this phantom pain, he was impressed by the mystery of the human body. Well, it wasn't the body that was mysterious, he would think, as he stared at the stump where his left hand had been, it was the mind.

A shout came from the deck. Unashi raced up the ladder to find the other sailors pointing towards the sea. 'Someone jumped off the cliff!'

'Get us closer!' the helmsman shouted.

As there were no winds, the sailors began to row, slowly nudging the ship forward. Unashi leant out over the gunwale and scanned the surface of the sea, luminous in the light of the full moon. He couldn't see anything. The water was still and the moonlight spread over it like oil. They pulled closer to the rugged limestone cliff that lay directly ahead. From the sea below, the cliff was immense. If someone fell from above it was unlikely they would survive, no matter how good a swimmer they were.

The sailors scanned the water, relying on the brilliance of the moonlight. No matter how dangerous the work aboard ship, they were always looking to protect the lives of others. If a shipmate fell into the sea, the other sailors would risk their own lives to rescue him.

'That's strange. Nothing has floated to the surface,' an old sailor said, shaking his head. 'After it sinks, a human body will eventually float up.'

'Then what could have happened?' Unashi asked.

'They jumped clutching a stone, perhaps,' the old sailor said.

If whoever had jumped was intent on suicide, there was little the sailors could do to help. Despair passed through the ship.

'This is a poor island, and I've heard that at times they thin the population.' The old sailor knitted his white brows.

'Something's floating!' One of the sailors had climbed to the lookout perch atop the mast of the mainsail. He was pointing at an object in the water. Just a little ahead, the sailors could see a white garment filled with air. The body was floating face up.

'A woman,' the sailors murmured.

When he heard it was a woman, an unpleasant sensation washed over Unashi. 'How can they tell it's a woman?'

'Men float face down, women face up,' a sailor answered, with lore gleaned from years at sea.

'Could a woman have jumped from a height like that?' The sailors grew animated, wondering what had happened. Their curiosity was half driven by pity and half by interest over what woman would have such courage – and what she might look like.

The old sailor and Unashi lowered a skiff over the gunwale and climbed into it. The old sailor rowed until he'd brought them alongside the corpse and Unashi reached out to it with a long hooked pole. He could now see that she was beautiful, with hair reaching down to her waist. Her features were finely formed and there wasn't so much as a mark on her white skin. Her lips were parted, making it seem as though she were smiling. Her legs had been bound at the ankles with rope, but the rope had snapped. Perhaps it had been tied to a stone when she had jumped but the impact of the fall had torn the rope.

'But this is Kamikuu!' the old sailor cried.

Startled, Unashi stared again at the woman's face. He remembered the name – Child of Gods. The old man had claimed earlier that she was the most beautiful woman in all the island chain, prettier even than Masago. And now that he saw her he had to agree. Her body, too, was exquisite. And yet she was dead.

'Something catastrophic must have happened to cause the great Oracle to take her own life, poor woman.'

The old sailor's voice was full of dismay as he gazed at Kamikuu's face. Unashi's phantom pain had vanished but he felt that, here, another danger – quite unlike that on Amaromi Island – awaited him. He looked towards the black outline of the island with misgivings.

Back aboard the ship they covered Kamikuu's corpse with a spare sail and laid her out upon the deck while they awaited daybreak. Everyone regarded the body with the deepest respect, but Unashi and the old sailor lingered alongside her, unable to quiet their agitation. How uncanny that the two women reputed to have been the most beautiful in all of the islands had died within a year. Was Kamikuu also a victim of Izanami's revenge? And, if so, what connected the two women? And why did Unashi feel he had been called to this island?

'The others are saying she was the great Oracle of the island,' the helmsman said to the old sailor, as he bowed before the corpse.

'She was.' The old man nodded. 'Some time ago I told Yakinahiko that the most beautiful woman in all the islands lived on this island – the great Oracle, Kamikuu.'

'Didn't you also tell Yakinahiko about the wasp that took passage on our ship? Do you remember, Unashi?'

Unashi answered, 'Yes. You let the wasp travel with you from Yamato to Nahariha.'

'Around the same time we heard that someone on Umihebi Island was stung to death by a wasp. Later I learnt that the man who died was the husband of this woman here.'

The sailors who had gathered at the deck exchanged glances. This coincidence portended bad luck.

'First Masago-sama, then Yakinahiko-sama, and now Kamikuu-sama. Since the night when we celebrated with *sake* and stories, each one has died. And all because we gave passage to a wasp that could understand human speech. Am I wrong? Or am I making too much of this?' the helmsman asked, as if to himself, as he rubbed his balding pate.

'I feel a strange premonition. We should not draw closer to the island,' a middle-aged sailor said, folding his brawny arms across his chest.

'But what about Kamikuu-sama? We can't just put her body into the ocean,' the helmsman shouted.

'Helmsman, her spirit lingers. She'll hear you.'

Superstitious, the sailors believed that, even after a person died, their spirit hovered for a while. Each man cast nervous glances – keeping watch over the dark seas and the corners of the deck. Someone muttered, 'It's bad luck to bring a woman aboard ship.'

'Helmsman, first thing tomorrow let's take the body ashore and then set sail.'

'That's for the best. Something's not right with this island.'

The drowning had lessened everyone's enthusiasm for going ashore. The sailors carried Kamikuu's corpse, draped tightly in the spare sail, to the bow of the ship. To avoid sight of it, they clustered together in the aft of the ship, sitting with their backs to the bow. Only Unashi and the old sailor remained seated near the body.

'I wonder if Kamikuu-sama gave up after her husband was killed by that wasp.' The old sailor's voice was choked with sighs. Could she have loved her husband so much she couldn't bear the pain of losing him? Unashi remembered the words the original Unashi had spoken. 'I will gladly give my life for you. And if Masago-hime knew that her death was the result of her association with you, I'm sure she would feel content. That's what love is. And you, too – you loved Masago-hime body and soul. That was what you told me yesterday.' Unashi gave himself over to his reveries.

The old sailor squinted. 'Anyway, we had a good time

that night Yakinahiko gave us *sake*. Happy memories like that are rare.'

If you live only once, then a happy moment is particularly prized. The dead priestess must also have had moments of intense joy as well as sorrow. Unashi could just see the tips of her white fingers from beneath the sail that covered her body. Her hands were curled, as if she were clutching something.

6

The next morning the helmsman called Unashi to him. Because the sailors had decided not to dock, the ship would wait in the offing for the small skiff to make land and return. Unashi and the old sailor had been selected to carry Kamikuu ashore. The crew of the ship would be in trouble if, for some unforeseen reason, someone on the island tried to steal their spare sail, so they placed Kamikuu in the skiff covered only with the torn robes she'd been wearing when she had leapt from the cliff. One of the sailors, influenced by the talk of the night before, edged to the side of the ship as the body was lowered into the skiff and, straddling the gunwale, sprinkled handfuls of their precious salt to purify the site.

The harbour on Umihebi Island made use of a natural inlet so there was no wharf. It looked as though it would easily flood when a storm arose. A single boat was moored there now – a dugout that would be used for collecting small fish and gathering seaweed. Since there were no other boats in sight, it seemed likely that the menfolk were at sea, fishing. Morning glories and hibiscus bloomed in profusion along the white sandy beaches. But the women and children, clutching baskets and searching the shores for shellfish and seaweed, were dressed in rags.

'The island's poor.' The old sailor stood up in the skiff and surveyed the land ahead. 'Wood for building must be hard to come by. They may be able to grow oaks, but they don't have much land here. Without forests they can't build large ships or houses.'

'But it is beautiful, isn't it?' Unashi took delight in the vista spread before him, as if he were gazing over Paradise. The old sailor glanced down at Kamikuu's corpse. Her hair had been arranged by the men and her hands folded together.

'It is. And being here at the easternmost corner of the island chain they claim it's sacred. In the morning when the sun rises, it seems to pass right through the island, so they say this is where the gods descend from the heavens. But now that the priestess who presides over the sun has died, I have no idea what the islanders will do.'

The women and children on the island caught sight of the skiff carrying the old sailor and Unashi. They seemed to have noticed the corpse as well because they began to clamour and scream. Young mothers grabbed their children's hands and fled the beach. A number of middle-aged women gathered their courage and nervously made their way to the skiff.

'Last night we saw this woman leap from the cliffs,' Unashi called.

The women rushed towards him, their faces full of alarm. 'It's Kamikuu-sama!'

Instantly the beach erupted with wailing. Unashi and the old sailor lifted Kamikuu's corpse from the skiff and laid it in the shade of a large tree. The white robes that had been soaked with sea water were now dry, and the hem fluttered in the ocean breeze. Her face was so peaceful in death that she looked as though she'd fallen asleep beneath the tree.

'Mother!'

Children raced across the sands, so frantic they could barely keep from stumbling. Surely they were Kamikuu's. A young woman was clutching a twin under each arm, a little girl of six or seven, and a boy who seemed at least ten. They were more comely than the others on the island – not surprising in Kamikuu's offspring – but, like the others, their clothing revealed their poverty.

'Are you the priestess's daughter?'

When the old sailor asked, the woman clutching the babies nodded.

'Where's your husband?'

'He put out to sea yesterday with my younger brother. He would never have believed this. What happened?'

'I can only tell you what we saw. Last night we were anchored in the inlet and we saw someone leap from the cliff. We rushed to rescue her, but the cliff is just too high, the waters too deep, and we couldn't get there in time. When we pulled the body from the sea we discovered that she was the high priestess of this island. I am so sorry we were not able to save her.'

As Unashi spoke, those gathered on the beach turned to stare at him. Whenever someone noticed that his left hand was missing, they glanced away. On most islands in the region, a man with no hand would become the subject of jokes and derision. The people on Umihebi Island might have been poor, but they were courteous and proud. Their island was sacred. Unashi sensed this and was moved by it.

'Thank you for your trouble.' Kamikuu's daughter spoke with composure. Her little sister had begun to whimper, so she stroked her cheek, then sat down beside her mother's corpse, her face filled with despair. The twins she cradled in her arms were still infants. Her attention to them and her sorrow over her mother made her seem very tired.

Word of Kamikuu's death spread, and before long an

old man, who seemed to be the island chief, and his attendants appeared on the beach.

'Let's be on our way now, Unashi,' the old sailor said, as he prepared to leave. He clearly wanted to avoid any trouble, but the women around him began to plead.

'Stay a little longer. The men left yesterday and it'll be some time before they return. Men have to carry the coffin. That is our custom. We won't be able to hold Kamikuu-sama's funeral with no men.'

Kamikuu must have considered that there would be no men to carry her coffin and had hoped to weigh her body down with the stone. If she had worried about what would happen after her death, why had she killed herself? Unashi was now eager to find out more.

'Unashi, we must go back to the ship,' the old sailor urged.

But Unashi did not move. 'If they need help with the coffin, I'll stay.'

'I'll tell the helmsman to wait a day. We'll come for you tomorrow at this time.'

The old sailor turned the skiff and rowed towards the trawler.

★

The chief of Umihebi Island was nearly eighty years old. He had a number of men assisting him, all of about the same age. Once a man was too old to fish, he took responsibility for the governance of the island.

'So it's come to this. Kamikuu-sama has died as well.' The island chief's eyes were milky. But it seemed he could see perfectly well, as he scowled down at Kamikuu's face. 'Her daughter gave birth to twins so we will not need to worry about her successor.'

The old men began to deliberate as they stood in front of Kamikuu's corpse. Her children sat alongside her, staring into space.

'Are you all right?' Unashi asked the eldest daughter.

She nodded listlessly. It seemed that since she had learnt her mother had committed suicide, she was unable to either speak or cry.

'I heard others saying that the man who was stung and killed by the wasp was your father. Is that true?'

'Yes,' she whispered. 'That was about a year and a half ago. My mother seemed to have a deeper understanding about what had happened, because afterwards she behaved strangely.'

'A deeper understanding?'

'After it happened, she stopped caring about her duties as priestess and just wandered along the beach. The island chief had to remind her that she had work to do. My father's death was too hard for her to accept. He and she had been so close. And then I gave birth to these twin girls three months ago. On our island fate determines the succession of *yin* and *yang*, dark and light, so when I gave birth to twins we had successors for the *yin* and *yang* roles. My mother rejoiced to know she had someone to take her place. Perhaps that was why she took her life – because she had no need to worry about it any more.'

'Aren't wasps unusual on this island?'

The woman nodded. 'The wasp stung my father between the eyes and then it died, too. I'd never seen anything like it on the island before. It must have flown in and just happened to sting my father. After he was stung my father's face swelled but he lived on for another half-day. Eventually it was so hard for him to breathe that he died. He was in agony. My mother was distraught. And now she is dead, too. I wonder if my family is cursed.' Tears began to roll down her cheeks.

'I'm sure that's not so.'

Unashi tried to comfort the young woman, but she continued, her expression grave. 'If it's decided that our family is cursed, we'll be ostracised from the community. My father's family was ostracised until his younger sister Yayoi was born.'

Kamikuu's daughter was terrified of rumours that might lead to her family's ostracism. Any family ostracised on such a small island would have a very difficult time surviving.

'I didn't mean to upset you.' Unashi surreptitiously observed Kamikuu's eldest daughter. Kamikuu had been *yang* – the principle of light and sun – and, true to form, her daughter, who would be *yin*, was her exact opposite. She was very plain and serious. Her younger sister was the same. Succession to the priesthood was determined by blood, and you could tell at a glance that they shared the same blood.

A group of women returned carrying a coffin. They gathered up Kamikuu's body and tried to settle it inside, but the coffin, made of the schima evergreen, was cheaply constructed and a size too small. They bent Kamikuu's legs and managed to wedge her inside. The island chief, who was slight in build, said he had had the coffin made for himself. How sad that Kamikuu was not to have a newly hewn one.

Throughout the island people were in tears. Perhaps because the menfolk were all away, Kamikuu's eldest daughter, her second daughter and even her taciturn second son drew next to Unashi and stayed close beside him as if he were their elder brother.

A woman on the brink of old age ran to them, gasping for breath, wearing hastily assembled white mourning robes. She had a string of pearls around her neck and carried a white shell. She began to chant a prayer and urged the others to stand up and join her.

The island chief, leaning on his cane, was at the head of the procession. Kamikuu's coffin was behind him. Unashi, an outsider, was clearly the youngest and strongest among the men. He carried the front of the coffin. The rest of the men had been left behind when the fishermen had set off. A middle-aged man seemed to be convalescing from a broken leg. Otherwise there were the three older men who attended the chief, and they were all in their eighties. Kamikuu's son, who was barely ten years old, stood alongside Unashi and tried to help carry the coffin.

The older woman who had been thrust into Kamikuu's role walked beside the coffin and sang what must have been a funeral dirge. She was unused to her position as high priestess and clearly uncomfortable. Her lack of poise did little to instil confidence in those around her. The funeral procession listlessly inched its way forward. The islanders, sunk in grief, made their way past one hut after another, each one so decrepit it seemed to have been dug out of the earth. Whenever they passed one, its occupants would emerge and join the end of the procession. Without thinking, Unashi glanced into a hut and was dismayed by how impoverished the islanders were. He'd seen enough. He kept his eyes downcast, the colour drained from his face.

Today, this very day
In the garden of the gods they hide;
In the garden of the gods they take pleasure;
In the garden of the gods they tarry;
From the heavens one descends,
From the seas one rises.
For today, this very day,
They pray.

Unashi looked back at Kamikuu's young son. He barely came to Unashi's chest and he was gritting his teeth from the strain of carrying the coffin.

'Are you all right?' Unashi asked.

The boy nodded unconvincingly.

'That's my mother's place,' he muttered miserably.

'I see. Is that woman a priestess, too?'

'She's my mother's deputy. The second priestess is supposed to come from the Umigame family – my father's family – but his sister Yayoi is already the priestess of the darkness, and there's no one else. The next in line is the Namako family. This woman's from that family. But she's not very good at chanting prayers and she can't dance.'

The priestess coughed and stammered her way through the prayer. As they listened to her voice, annoyingly off key, the islanders carried the heavy coffin and slowly headed west.

'Where are we going?' Unashi asked.

The boy had barely enough breath to answer, but he managed, 'To the Amiido. The burial ground. Where the caves are.' Many of the islanders in the archipelago interred their dead in caves.

Circumstances had pressed Unashi into service as a bearer of the dead, but he wondered what had really drawn him here. There had to be a reason, and until he found out what it was, he would not leave.

> *O great Oracle,*
> *Thou hast hidden;*
> *O blessed sisters,*
> *Both are hidden.*

When they had walked a little over a mile, they came to a cape on what must have been the westernmost point of the island. The boy was so tired he could hardly speak. Midway another old man had joined the procession and had helped to carry the coffin, relieving him. The boy had taken his little sister by the hand and stuck close to Unashi.

'That's the Amiido there.'

Unashi could see a dark opening along one side of the dense thicket of pandan and banyan trees. The trees formed a natural tunnel, through which the path continued. It grew so narrow in the tunnel that the coffin barely squeezed through and members of the funeral procession had to follow one another in single file. Eventually it opened on to a wide, circular, grassy area. Across the circle Unashi saw a large cave in the limestone cliff. Deep inside it there were rows of coffins. Next to the cave stood a small, ramshackle hut with a pandan-thatched roof. Perhaps the keeper of the burial ground lived there.

When he looked closer, he saw a young woman standing in the shadows cast by the hut, crying. She was tall, and even though he had never seen her before, she seemed somehow familiar. Her brows curved in pretty arches and her eyes, full of wisdom, sparkled with youthful vitality. Unashi had meant to steal just a glance at her, but once he saw her face, he was transfixed. For her part, however, she took no notice of him and wiped away her tears with the sleeves of her ragged garment.

'Who is the woman over there?' Unashi asked the boy at his side, his heart already captivated.

'That's Yayoi, priestess of the darkness.'

Priestess of the day and priestess of the darkness. So, she was the younger sister of Kamikuu's husband, the man who'd been stung by the wasp. He knew immediately that he – Yakinahiko – had come to life as the nineteen-year-old Unashi solely to meet this woman. It was for her that he had been guided to Umihebi Island. An invincible love took hold of his heart – so strong he found it difficult to breathe. And the joy that welled within him was so intense he wanted to leap and shout, regardless of the fact that he was in the midst of a funeral. Truly this is what it means to be alive! he thought, as he gazed at the stump of his left hand.

The island chief gave instructions for the placement of the coffin, then Unashi and the old men carried it into the cave. The newer coffins were close to the entrance. Those that were deeper within were rotten and white bones jutted over the edges. Unashi imagined that Kamikuu's husband's body was in one of the newer ones. After they had settled the coffin in its place and left the cave, Unashi caught the eye of Yayoi, who was walking towards him. 'How comely now the woman.' The ancient phrase had leapt to his lips. Those were words Izanaki had once spoken to Izanami. 'Ah, might this be a good woman?'

Of course, Yayoi did not know who Unashi was and she shot him a suspicious look. Her reaction was not un-expected. She had encountered someone from a completely different world. But what Unashi did not fail to notice was that her surprise at seeing him was accompanied by an attraction to this young and handsome man. 'Let's run away to a different, distant world!' Unashi shouted to Yayoi in his heart. 'Let's leave this island.' Yayoi stared at him quizzically. 'Did you hear what I said?' Unashi shouted again, silently. Yayoi was still looking directly at him. He thought she must have caught a glimpse of the love burning inside him. She must have seen that, although this was the first time they had met, it was for this meeting that they had both been living. For this very moment.

'Yayoi,' the island chief called, and she moved towards him. 'It happened so suddenly that we had no time to prepare another coffin. We will start working on it now, so I want you to drink this by tomorrow morning.'

Yayoi took the earthenware vessel that the chief handed to her. It seemed to contain liquid. Sensing a collective sigh of sorrow, Unashi looked around him. The islanders who had accompanied the funeral procession were all weeping silently. He turned to the boy and asked, 'What's this?'

The boy began to cry so hard he could barely speak. Tears were also streaming down the cheeks of Kamikuu's eldest daughter, and she was unable to lift her head. Because their grief had intensified so suddenly, Unashi could only predict that some new tragedy awaited them.

Once the chief had handed Yayoi the earthenware vessel, the other members of the funeral procession prepared to depart, as though their business at the Amiido had ended. They withdrew from the grassy space, leaving Yayoi without a word of farewell. Unashi hurried after them. But the thought of Yayoi left alone in that eerie place was almost more than he could bear. He decided that he would bide his time and, once night fell, he would return.

'What happens next?' he asked the boy, who was plodding wearily along. Everyone was going their separate ways and returning to their houses.

'All the islanders will come to our house, so they're going home now to prepare the food.'

'What about Yayoi?'

The boy stopped. 'Usually, the priestess of the

darkness is not allowed to see anyone until the mourning is over. She lives among the dead.'

'But this time it's different.'

The boy stammered, 'I don't really know.'

Unashi wanted to return to the Amiido and speak to Yayoi. But the timing did not seem right. Instead he continued to walk with Kamikuu's family to their late mother's house. They crossed the island and made their way to the cape on the eastern side where she had had her prayer hall and living quarters. When they reached the cape, Unashi looked over the edge of the cliff to the sea below. He wanted to make sure his ship was still anchored in the offing. It also occurred to him that it was from this point that Kamikuu had leapt to her death.

As the sun set the islanders began their simple funerary feast. They set out shellfish and seaweed dishes. To accompany the *sake*, they served dried fish fin that had been heated over the fire. The *sake* was brewed from fermented rice. Unashi took a sip. His throat had been so dry that the *sake* tasted delicious.

'We're very grateful to you, sir,' the island chief began. 'Thanks to you, Kamikuu-sama was able to return home and now we can move on to the next generation.' The other elderly men and the women he had helped offered their thanks as well.

'What happens now?' Unashi asked.

The chief looked up with his filmy eyes, and said, 'When Kamikuu-sama dies, then the priestess of the darkness dies, too. Kamikuu-sama took her own life because the custom distressed her. If her body hadn't been discovered, we wouldn't have known if she were dead or not and we couldn't have proceeded. But because you pulled the body out of the water and brought it home, we can appoint a new priestess. The twin girls you see over there will succeed her when they turn sixteen. Until then, we will make do with temporary priestesses. Kamikuu-sama was very vivacious and her successor will be a little less so. It'll offer a change in mood.'

'And why does Yayoi have to die?' Unashi asked.

'On our island day is paired with night and *yang* with *yin*. That is why.'

Unashi understood that it wasn't to spare the island a funeral but to spare Yayoi from death that Kamikuu had killed herself. In retrieving her body and carrying it back to the island, they had transgressed. When Unashi realized that this meant Yayoi might be dying at that very minute, he leabut up from his seat in such a state of agitation that he lost his balance and fell.

7

He lay unconscious for some time in a corner of the room. When he came to, he stretched out his right hand and patted the air around him to be sure no one else was there. He was relieved to discover that he was still in the room where they had held the wake. He was able to pull himself to his feet. But when he did so his head began to throb. A stranger to the island, he was not used to its *sake* and it had had a near narcotic effect on him. He remembered the old shaman who had told him that different islands had different poisons so he was happy to be awake again. Feeling his way, Unashi found the door and let himself out of the room. He made his way to the well, rinsed his mouth and drank.

The moon was listing in the west. Dawn was near. Unashi managed to press ahead, his legs wobbly. He wanted to hurry and was frustrated when his body refused to co-operate. When he'd been Yakinahiko, the shaman in the village where everyone had worn the shell armlets had told him, 'Throughout those islands there are poisons we don't have in Yamato.'

Now he understood that the shaman's words pointed to Yayoi and her destiny.

It took nearly an hour but he finally reached the path that led to the Amiido. He could hear people speaking in hushed voices. A number of elderly islanders were standing at the entrance whispering and peering into the tunnel of trees ahead of them. Night-watchmen! They were taking turns to guard the entrance, making sure Yayoi did not try to escape. What a terrifying island this was. If he were caught, they wouldn't hesitate to use the poison on him. But he couldn't give up now. He began making his way to the western shore. He would have to scale the cliff and enter the Amiido from the other side. The sky was gradually brightening towards the east making it easier to climb. For all he knew, Yayoi was already dead.

Once he had scaled the cliff, he manoeuvred until he was directly above the burial cave. He could see the little hut beside it and it seemed that a light was lit within it. There was still time. He scampered down the embankment and drew alongside the hut, where he called to her softly, 'Yayoi!'

The door opened slightly, and Yayoi peered out. Her

eyes were swollen from crying. Unashi gave a sigh of relief, and reached for her hand. But Yayoi spoke fearfully. 'Who are you?'

'Quick – we have no time to lose. We must flee.'

'But how?' Yayoi's voice was desperate, nearly a wail, and sharp enough to cut through the trees sheltering the entrance to the Amiido. The old people waiting there would likely think it signalled the moment of her death. But Unashi recognised in her voice a fierce anger. She wanted to live. She wanted to flee to another world and give herself to love. More than anything, her voice registered the anger she felt at being forced to cut her life short. Perhaps, when he had seen her earlier that day, he had conveyed his feelings to her.

Yayoi squeezed Unashi's right hand. Hers was trembling a little. 'It's too late. This island is small and there's no way off it. The old people are keeping watch at the entrance. And beyond that, as far as The Warning stone, the path is covered with a thicket of thorns. No one has ever gone past The Warning. I hear that you can go to the northern cape, but without a boat, you cannot get off the island. So, you see, escape is impossible.'

'What did you say was past The Warning stone?'

Yayoi looked up at the sky anxiously, then pointed towards the north. 'I've been told there's a tunnel through the thorny pandan thickets. But only the high priestess may take the path. No one else may go there so I've never seen it. But I've heard it said that if you get through the pandan you will come out at the northern cape.'

'The northern cape? Then I will have you wait for me there. I'm going back to the wharf to steal the dugout I saw there. Then I'll head north.'

'I don't know if I can do that by myself.'

'If you stay here you'll have to take the poison and die. You'll end up in the coffin next to Kamikuu – as young as you are. Come – choose life. Choose me.'

Unashi pulled Yayoi into his arms and embraced her tightly. The brusque suddenness of it caused her to stiffen instinctively. Unashi held her chin firmly with his right hand and brought his lips to hers. He breathed life into her. He had once been a god. But a human – a man whose lifespan is finite and limited – had given him the precious gift of life. Unashi closed his eyes. He would hold on to Yayoi's life.

Yayoi noticed that his left hand was missing. 'What happened to you?' she asked.

'A snake bite.'

She kept her eyes fixed on Unashi, took his left arm and brought the stump gently to her cheek. 'Let me be your left hand.'

It was now clear that he had been guided here so that he could meet this woman. Unashi felt calm. He pushed firmly on Yayoi's back. 'Hurry. We must be off this island before day has broken completely. People will begin moving around soon.'

Yayoi ran towards the north, her gait nimble. Once she was through the Amiido thickets and past The Warning, there was just one road she could travel. It was the only way to escape. She looked back at Unashi nervously. He waved her on. And then he went to find the dugout.

He had to hurry. Once again he scaled the wall of the cliff and went down to the beach. This time he climbed from a different spot. He moved south-east, towards the port, remaining under the cover of the trees. As soon as it grew light enough, the women on the island would be out combing the sands for shellfish and seaweed. He had to steal the boat before they reached the beach. The ship he had sailed in was still anchored in the offing. But not for much longer. He needed to pick up Yayoi from the northern cape and take her with him to the ship.

There were already people on the beach – the middle-aged women who had put Kamikuu's body in the coffin. Worse, they had pulled the dugout on to the beach, and were standing around it, talking.

'Hello!' Unashi called.

The women looked up in surprise as he appeared out of nowhere.

'Will you lend me the dugout?'

The women shook their heads. 'The chief told us to make a coffin with it. We've had it up here during the night to dry.'

'Whose coffin?'

The women looked down and said nothing. Yayoi's suicide was clearly a taboo topic. They expected her to die quietly, alone.

'If you need to make a coffin, it's better to cut down a tree. If you tear up this dugout you won't have a single boat left on the island. Then what will you do?'

Unashi stared at the women. They glanced at one another in confusion.

'I need to see my shipmates about some business. Can't you lend me the boat for just a little while? I promise to bring it back. Please, won't you help me? I'll return with gifts for you.'

'Well, if you could bring us back some grain . . .' a woman said timidly.

Another joined in: 'I'll take some cloth. I don't care what kind of cloth . . . we're so poor here.'

'And you?'

When Unashi asked the last woman she looked perplexed, then blurted, 'I'd like that skiff you were riding.'

'So you had better wait to make the coffin.'

The women helped Unashi push out to sea. Finally he was on his way. He cast a sideways glance at the shell trawler, anchored in the offing, and began to paddle towards the northern cape with his one arm. The current was swift, and his progress was slow, but he reached his goal as day was breaking. Yayoi had not arrived. He wondered if she'd been caught, and watched for her anxiously.

The northern cape was rocky and there was no place for him to pull ashore. If he let the boat drift too close to the rocks, the waves would break the dugout in two. As he scanned the coastline for a place to dock, the morning sun began to rise in the sky. Yayoi still had not come. With morning the island chief and the others would go to the Amiido to make sure that she had killed herself. Once they discovered she'd escaped, the island would be in uproar. Had she already been caught? If not, then where was she? And if she took much longer, someone from the trawler would be coming ashore to look for him, exposing their plot.

Just then Yayoi stepped out of the pandan thicket. She was visibly relieved when she caught sight of Unashi, and wiped away the sweat that was dripping from her brow. Her legs were bare, scratched and bleeding, but she ran towards Unashi joyfully, her eyes shining. Unashi waved his right arm to show her the way to go, but Yayoi had already leapt into the sea, quick-witted enough to chart her own course. She swam to him and grabbed the edge of the dugout. When Unashi pulled her in, it rocked violently. Yayoi, drenched to the bone, picked up the other oar and began to paddle.

'You must be cold in your wet clothes.'

'I just want to get away from the island as quickly as possible.'

'This is the only boat there is. They can't get us now.'

Yayoi sighed with relief and looked back at the northern cape. Seen from the sea, the cliffs were sheer, and along the walls pure white trumpet lilies bloomed. 'That's strange. I've never looked at the island from the sea. I never knew it had such an interesting shape – or that it was so small!' She looked into Unashi's face. 'Who *are* you?'

'My name is Unashi.'

'Where are you from?'

'Yamato.'

'What kind of place is it?'

'It's beautiful, but it has poisons that you don't have here.'

When she heard Unashi's answer, Yayoi turned her face towards the morning sun. It was higher now, and it painted her lovely face the colour of a mandarin orange. Unashi was dazzled.

'There is always poison. You can be certain of it. So long as there is a day, there will be a night. And where there is *yang*, there is *yin*. To every front, a back. No white without black. Everything on earth has its opposite, its mate. Should you wonder why, if there were only one there'd be no birth. In the beginning there were two, and those two were attracted to one another and drew together, and from there we have meaning. Or so it is said.'

'You learnt that from someone?'

'From Kamikuu-sama. Recently she had lost interest in life but she spent time telling me many things. That she chose to die as she did makes me so sad.'

Tears rolled down Yayoi's cheeks as the memories came back to her.

'Why did Kamikuu-sama kill herself?'

'Probably because she could not bear to continue since she was living such a lie.' Yayoi's face clouded.

'What do you mean?'

'Kamikuu-sama's husband was named Mahito. And he said he was my elder brother. But when he was stung by that wasp he confessed a number of things to Kamikuu-sama just before he died. He told her that I was the child he had had with Kamikuu-sama's younger sister. That made me Kamikuu-sama's niece – which meant I was *yang*. And yet Mahito had told the island chief that I was his younger sister, which made me a daughter in the family of the auxiliary priestess. So I became the next priestess of the darkness. Everyone thought it was my fate, decided from ancient times. But once I learnt the truth from Kamikuu-sama, I couldn't bear it any more. I am so grateful to you for rescuing me.'

Yayoi wiped the tears that had spilt with the back of her hands. Unashi took her wet hands in his. 'And what became of your mother?'

'My mother's name was Namima. She was Kamikuu-sama's younger sister, so that meant she was *yin* and destined to become the priestess of the darkness. But, she became pregnant with me and fled the island with my father. I heard that they slipped away in a little boat very much like the one we are in now. My mother gave birth to me aboard the boat. And then she died.'

'Did she die in childbirth?'

'No. My father never explained it very clearly. But Kamikuu-sama always suspected that my father killed my mother. My father wanted to be with Kamikuu-sama and he wanted to help his family escape their curse so he brought me back to the island with him. If he killed Namima, I can't imagine Kamikuu-sama would ever have forgiven him.'

'Another story of betrayal.' Unashi had spoken to himself, but Yayoi stared at him uncertainly.

'Have you also been betrayed?'

Unashi gazed at the shell trawler and did not answer. If he made Yayoi his wife, how would Izanami react? He lost himself in his thoughts. Once she realised that Unashi was really Izanaki, she would kill Yayoi. It was inevitable.

What if he made his way down the Yomotsuhira-saka, the Yomi Slope, and met Izanami? Perhaps they could come to a new understanding. But now that he was a human being, where would he find the power to accomplish such a feat? He could not truly know love without being human. And he had no extraordinary powers unless he was a god. How could he protect Yayoi?

Unashi concentrated on rowing the dugout, keeping a careful watch on Yayoi's profile. He had to come up with a plan.

HOW COMELY NOW THE MAN

1

I walked idly through the corridors in the underworld palace, my thoughts on Yayoi. I longed for her to be relieved of her fear and freed from the taint of defilement that was certain to burden her. But what could I do? I was dead. My impatience, my grief — impossible to resolve — only made the darkness surrounding me that much darker. Izanami had been right. I should never have turned into that wasp. How much better off I'd be now, not knowing of Yayoi's miserable fate.

I saw Mahito lurking in the shadows of one of the tall pillars. Of course, it wasn't really Mahito, just the filmy outline of a hollow spirit that vaguely resembled the man he'd once been. The sight of him upset me. It wasn't that he didn't remember killing me, or even that he'd forgotten all the lies he had told, but seeing him like that made me all the more aware of the emptiness of the dead. And it reminded me afresh of the unbearable pain I had endured. The daughter that we had had together was still on that island, now the priestess of the darkness. Once I had discovered that she had taken my place in a fate I had found so unbearable, I could find no rest. And my agitation grew all the greater when I learnt that Mahito had done as he had in order to rescue his own family from their plight. This had allowed him to marry Kamikuu, the woman he had loved and who had loved him since childhood. My thoughts went round and round until they had wound themselves into hatred.

It was death that gave birth to my hatred. Until then I had never realised just how much energy hatred gave the dead. And no matter how hard I tried, I could not resign myself to my fate. Why had things happened as they had? I could not help but blame Mahito. I had always felt a certain sympathy for Izanami but in the beginning I hadn't appreciated the depth of her hatred. Once I knew the extent of Mahito's betrayal, I felt I understood to my very core the true import of Izanami's feelings. And surely that was why I was in the Realm of the Dead.

Today, like all other days, Mahito stared into the darkness with the same listless expression. Clearly he still didn't understand what had happened to him, why he was in the Realm of the Dead, or the kind of being he had become. He was a wandering spirit, doomed for ever to this existence of restless sorrow. Poor pathetic Mahito. Somehow, I thought, he resembled me. True, I had had no idea when I fled Umihebi Island with him that this fate awaited us.

'Hello, Mahito.'

When I greeted him, Mahito bowed politely without glancing at me. He looked like a forlorn child, searching the perpetual darkness for a familiar face, too frightened to let his gaze linger on anything for long. When I drew nearer to him, I could see a small scar between his brows. I pointed to it and asked, 'What happened there?' though I already knew the answer.

Mahito brought his hand to his forehead and touched the scar with his finger. Perplexity spread over his face. 'I don't know.'

'It looks a little swollen. It must have hurt.'

Mahito covered his brow with his hand, as if trying to hide the scar. 'I don't remember.'

'Didn't a wasp sting you?' I persisted. It looked as though he didn't want to remember what had happened in the living world. And it irritated me that his memory was so unlike my own. Ever since I had turned into a wasp and had flown to Umihebi Island, I had become vicious.

'I don't remember.' Mahito averted his face, seemingly in great pain. He still did not realise that he was dead; he had lost his memory and he had become a timid man.

And I who died ahead of you have suffered so horribly. I grieved so much at being parted from you and our daughter. How I worried for you both! How much better it would have been for me to have had no feelings at all. But I was left to cry in utter despair in this never-ending darkness. I want you to feel all that I have felt.

I wanted to strike Mahito with the full force of my hatred – I could hardly restrain myself. 'Why don't you remember? Weren't you the one who strangled me to death when you decided you no longer had a use for me? And then you passed our daughter off as your sister. You forced her to become the priestess of the darkness, didn't you?'

'Did I?'

'Why would you ask such a thing? You were in love with Kamikuu – and you didn't want me.'

'Kamikuu is my wife, that much I know is true. As for the rest, I don't know what you're talking about.'

'I was Kamikuu's younger sister. My name is Namima.'

'I've heard that name before, but I can't place it.'

'You left the island with Namima, the priestess of the darkness. And then you killed her. You took Yayoi, the baby you had with her, back to the island and you told everyone she was your sister. You're a murderer!'

Mahito's lips quivered as he looked at me. I was sure

my eyes must have been like Izanami's, unfocused. As soon as he caught sight of them he averted his own, as if he had seen something he shouldn't have.

'I haven't killed anyone. I did return to the island with a baby. But that's all I remember.'

'You're lying! She was ours. We gave her the name Yayoi.'

Mahito only remembered what pleased him. Suddenly he brought his hands to his face and cowered. The gloom beneath the pillars grew darker and more oppressive. The other spirits in the hall sympathised with him, knowing he had lost sight of himself. They, too, felt my anger as I stood there, a malevolent spirit in human form. But no one understood my pain. At that moment I realised I was utterly alone – dejected and forlorn.

'When you died, how did you feel?' I pressed on with my questions.

'It hurt.' He began to shake as he remembered the pain of death. 'My face swelled. I lost my sight, and it grew harder to breathe until finally I couldn't breathe at all. I didn't know what was happening to me. But the pain was there to the bitter end.'

'It serves you right.'

'Such a cruel thing to say.' Mahito's shoulders sank.

'How do you feel now, being here?'

'I'm worried about my family. Our island is so poor. I have to catch as many fish as I can to trade for rice. What will they do now?'

The things we do are so futile, so ugly. Mahito wasn't going to remember anything, no matter how hard I pushed him. How would I dispel my hatred? I wanted to be one of those drifting spirits, floating aimlessly, remembering nothing.

'Namima?'

I saw a form coming towards me, silhouetted by pale blue light. Izanami had entered the hall.

'I'm here.'

Mahito looked at her, his face full of fear. He tried to hide in the shadow of the pillar. Not being of flesh and blood, there was little he could do to tether himself. I stopped talking to him and waited for Izanami.

'What have you been doing?'

'I've been tormenting Mahito.'

Izanami's brows were pulled together in her usual frown, but now she looked even unhappier than usual. 'Namima, you've changed of late. That man has no memory of you.'

'Izanami-sama, I want to make him suffer. I don't think he should be allowed to forget.' I had begun to cry. My cheeks felt strangely warm where the tears flowed. I hated being in this underworld hell. I blurted out, 'How can I continue in a place like this?'

Suddenly I was aware that I was standing before Izanami, the goddess who ruled the 'place like this'. 'Please forgive me!' I prostrated myself before her.

Izanami's face had clouded. When she finally spoke, she said, 'That's not why I came to find you. I have something to discuss with you.' She turned and walked towards the chamber where she decided whose turn it was to die. She sat on her granite chair.

'It appears Izanaki died not long ago.'

I was stunned. But then I saw that the glow of bitterness, which normally attended Izanami, was a little fainter today. Of course, Izanaki was a god. Could gods ever really die? True, Izanami was dead and now presiding over the Realm of the Dead. Did that mean Izanaki would make his way here? Surely not. I had heard that when gods died they rose up to the High Plain of Heaven. Izanami, then, was a goddess proud in her singularity.

'What has become of Izanaki-sama following his death?'

'I've no idea. He lived for a long time as a human named Yakinahiko. But apparently he was felled by the sword of his young retainer and this time he did not return to life. His goshawk watched it all unfold and took revenge on the retainer. But I do not know what happened after that.'

'Izanami-sama, how was it possible for Izanaki-sama to die? Could his retainer have been a man of such incredible strength?'

'I know none of the details.'

Izanami propped an elbow on her chair's armrest and put her chin in her hand. 'Maybe Izanaki grew tired of living. Maybe it was because he had to go from one woman to the next producing children, never knowing when it would all end.'

Her face was vacant. She was used to deciding daily who would die. But today, she did not seem interested in it. She had set the bowl – full of the black water drawn from the well – on the stone floor where it remained untouched.

I suddenly made a terrible discovery. Spurred by my hatred of Mahito, I found myself longing for someone to die. Wasn't this the feeling that had gripped Izanami when she was first locked up in the Realm of the Dead? Hatred is terrifying. I longed for someone to relieve me – I wrapped my arms around my body and trembled. 'Izanami-sama, I beg of you. I am so restless. I want to be just another spirit. I want to disappear into the darkness and spend my time in perfect silence. I want never to see Mahito's face again. I just want to forget everything. Please let me be a calm, quiet spirit. I've had more than enough of this suffering.'

I threw myself at Izanami's feet. She looked down at me gloomily.

'Namima, what is it that makes you suffer?'

'Just as it is for you, Izanami-sama. Bitterness and sorrow. I am full of bitterness towards Mahito. But I feel such sorrow for my daughter and the fate she faces. I want to rid myself of these feelings but I don't know how. And, Izanami-sama, I do not think you know either. I just want to be an ordinary dead person. Please, I beg of you, let me float off into the darkness.'

'Namima, I thought you were able to understand my suffering.'

'I fear you overestimate me. I am just a mediocre woman, tormented by jealousy.'

An icy silence froze between Izanami and myself. I had allowed myself to speak out of turn, and I knew I should prepare to be punished. If punishment meant I were to suffer a *real* death, how much the better it would be for me.

'Kamikuu is the name of the priestess of the day on your island, isn't it?'

I looked up at her in shock. That was not a name I

had expected her to utter. 'She was my sister, older than me by one year. Why do you ask?'

'It appears she has died.'

I could not believe my ears. My beautiful sister – always so dignified and majestic. No matter what challenges she encountered she always excelled. Not Kamikuu, not the great Oracle! She was the most important woman on the entire island – no wonder Mahito had been in love with her.

'How did she die?'

'It seems she threw herself from a cliff.'

I gasped. 'It must have been my fault. She must have despaired of living after I killed Mahito!'

'There's no point in trying to assess blame.' Izanami spoke as if the very idea were tiresome. 'Who can say whose fault it was?'

Even so, I couldn't help worrying. If Kamikuu had died, then Yayoi would have to die, too. What must Yayoi be feeling now as she confronted her fate? I asked Izanami, 'What has happened to Yayoi?'

'I have no idea. All I can say is that her spirit has not made its way here, so we can assume that, if she is dead, she died without regret.'

I was slightly mollified. Still, I couldn't help but reflect on the way my actions had affected the island – just like the ripples from a stone cast into water. I had turned into a wasp and killed Mahito. And once he had died, Kamikuu – realising the fickleness of the world – had killed herself.

'Izanami-sama, I have a request.'

Izanami turned back to me. I sensed her empty, unfocused eyes upon me as I straightened up to speak.

'Namima,' she snapped, 'if you're going to ask again to be allowed to become an ordinary spirit, the answer is no!'

'That's not it.'

'Then what is it?' She turned to face me squarely.

I spoke clearly and forcefully: 'I would like you to let me select the thousand who will die.' I thought I could see a smile curl along one corner of Izanami's lips. I suspected she meant to say, 'But you are human . . .' so I interjected: 'I hope that you will let me undertake the task, as your assistant. It seems simple enough. I draw the black water from the well behind the palace, then sprinkle it over the map. And by the mere flick of my wrist death is visited upon a thousand people.'

I wasn't afraid of Izanami or anything else. There was no punishment greater now than the bitterness I felt on seeing Mahito.

'Do you wish to become a god? Is that it, Namima? You'll become a god and do my work?'

Izanami spoke in a low voice I had not heard before.

It chilled me to the bone. I shook my head vigorously. 'No. I'm perfectly content to perform the deed as your priestess. Please just give me your command and I will begin. You must be exhausted, Izanami-sama, so let me select the thousand in your stead. Truly, no one understands you better than I do, Izanami-sama. Surely it would be permissible for you to allow me this one request.'

I must have sounded arrogant. The minute the words left my mouth I was cringing in horror at my temerity.

Izanami was silent.

Now that Kamikuu had died, wouldn't Yayoi soon make her way to this underground realm? But Yayoi would not know who I was – just as Mahito had not. She would float about, an empty spirit, causing me no end of torment. My whole life had been for naught. The thought was too painful to bear.

'What do you say to my request, Izanami-sama? What do you say?'

Once again I prostrated myself before her.

'Very well. Come this way.'

Izanami stood and moved towards the map of the world. The bowl of black water that one of the servants had prepared earlier waited in the middle of the floor.

'Sprinkle the water. Take the lives of a thousand people.'

She handed me the bowl. The daily death of a thousand people had been born of the battle between Izanami and Izanaki. It was meant as revenge, pure and simple, on a man who had tried to escape the defilement of death. I lifted the bowl to sprinkle the water but, try as I might, I could not bring myself to do it. I could not get over the fact that a thousand people would perish with but one flick of my wrist. At heart I was just too cowardly.

Suddenly I brought the bowl to my lips and drank the liquid. Of course, I couldn't actually drink since I was a spirit. It trickled out of my mouth and down my chin, staining my whole body black. I remembered how I had cried when Mikura-sama had said, 'It's because you're impure.' I had watched the tears trickle down my dirty bare legs. Now that I was dead, I could not die again, could I? Then how was I ever to escape my pain?

'Apparently, Namima, you can't do it.'

I had collapsed on the cold stone floor, but when I heard Izanami's voice, I pulled myself up. She was standing beside me.

'I'm sorry.'

'A human life means nothing to a god and can be taken away at will. But for you . . . you're human, and that makes you hesitate. Gods and humans are different. My suffering and yours are different.'

'Then, Izanami-sama, why do you suffer?' I asked, without thinking.

'Because I am a *female* god.' Izanami sent the servant back to the well for more water. Then, with no hesitation, she sprinkled it here and there – in complete disregard of the fact that Izanaki was no longer in the world of the living.

I looked down at my body, stained with the black water, and wondered what kind of pain a goddess had to bear. She had to steal life from the living, all the while in possession of her woman's heart. Was that the source of her pain? Or was it that while she was a goddess who killed she was also a female charged with giving birth? The more I thought about it, the more depressed I became, and the more I regretted my outburst. I understood that the suffering I endured as a human was nothing compared to that which Izanami bore.

I was utterly dejected. A spirit can't exactly fall ill, but all I wanted to do was float about, with no memory of life's pain, like Mahito. I didn't present myself to Izanami after that, and I did not come across Mahito. I spent my time wandering alone through the underworld darkness, praying that I might melt into the gloom.

One day, when I was walking along the dark tunnel, as was my wont, I felt a cool breeze pass across my cheek and turned to look behind me. No breezes ever blew in the Realm of the Dead. There was never any flow of air, so although the thick staleness occasionally wavered and swayed, it never dislodged itself. A persistent heaviness hung thickly wherever I went. It startled me, then, to feel a breeze.

'Namima.' It was Hieda no Are's voice.

'Are-san! When did you return?'

Hieda no Are walked briskly, her breath laboured. 'A little while ago. When I was travelling through Yamato somebody stepped on me and killed me. The life of an ant is brief indeed! But briefer still is a woman's fame, for history now remembers Hieda no Are as a man!'

She was even more talkative than before and full of energy.

'Namima, there's a man I don't know in the underground palace. Isn't he your husband? He reminds me of Umi-sachi-hiko and Yama-sachi-hiko. Do you remember? I told you about Ho-ori's poem, the one he sent to Princess Toyo-tama.'

Hieda no Are looked as if she were about to recite the poem again but I turned away. It was rude, I knew, but any mention of Mahito left me feeling gloomy. A startled look flashed across her face.

'This is serious indeed. We need to report immediately to Izanami-sama.'

'Report what?' I did not understand why Hieda no Are seemed so alarmed.

'The boulder blocking the Yomotsuhira Slope. A large party of sailors is trying to move it. Any minute now and they'll have pushed it back far enough for a man to enter. Someone may come in.'

That was the giant boulder Izanaki had thrown into the mouth of the cave, to separate the Realm of the Dead for ever from the world of the living. I had heard that the boulder was so heavy that even a thousand men could not move it. How was it possible that someone might enter? 'It is said that to human eyes our underground palace would look like nothing more than a vast tomb.'

'Listen. Someone's coming. Human beings are so full of curiosity. Who might it be?' Hieda no Are's voice was buoyant and bright.

Izanaki was the only person who had ventured all the way down into the Realm of the Dead. But Izanaki was a god. Human beings, by their very nature, were terrified of the immense subterranean crypt and glad to have the boulder just where it was. There was no reason for them to draw any closer than that.

2

I could see a wisp of light, barely visible, waving back and forth in the distance. It was coming towards me. Had the living finally pushed their way into this world – a world into which they should never trespass? Of course, Izanami and I were barely visible to living eyes. The light we cast was not even as bright as that of a firefly. And the other spirits melted into the surrounding darkness and were invisible. But if a person were brave enough to travel down into this underworld crypt, they would surely find the darkness here – packed to the brim with the spirits of the dead – so dense it was nearly suffocating.

That would be the least of their worries, though. I was more concerned with how Izanami would react and the anger she would unleash on any living creature impetuous enough to invade her sanctuary. Might she cause the ceiling to cave in, for instance, and trap the interloper for ever in her depths? And what kind of person was bold enough to trespass into her realm anyway?

In the distance I could hear the echo of a man's voice. 'Izanami, if you are here, won't you answer? It's Izanaki.'

The intruder wasn't human, after all. Izanaki, who was said to have died, had returned again to Yomi. Izanami spun round, her body as taut as a whip ready to snap, and stepped back.

'Izanami, where are you?'

'Here.' Her voice quivered. That was only natural. She was meeting the man from whom she had parted more than a thousand years ago at the Yomotsuhira-saka where together they had exchanged words that carried the full force of their bitter passion.

A warm light suddenly flooded the underground palace – the light from a thick pine torch. Until now the only illumination had been the pale will-o'-the-wisp light of ghostly spirits. The man holding the torch was unexpectedly young. His body, which had not yet filled out, was slender. His long hair was not pulled up in the two topknots that had once been the fashion but was tied with a leather thong at the back of his neck. His right arm was bound with a band of shell, and his white kimono was short. At his waist he wore a long sword, and he smelt of the sea – like the fishermen from my island.

'Izanami, it's Izanaki.'

'You've changed.' Izanami's voice still quivered. 'The

Izanaki I knew had the sturdy body of an older man. Even so, "How comely now the man."'

The young man who called himself Izanaki seemed to smile slightly. Suddenly I noticed that his left hand was missing.

'Izanami, won't you show yourself to me?' He sounded disconsolate.

'You can't see me?' Izanami asked with surprise.

'No.'

'Are you really Izanaki-sama?'

'I have transformed myself into a human being with an allotted time on earth. In a few decades I will die and then perhaps I, too, will come to this underworld of death. I wilfully abandoned myself as a god.'

'Why?'

'Because I could not bear outliving another wife. And that is why I've come here – I wish to apologise.'

Izanami gasped. What Izanaki had told her was not what she had expected.

Izanaki, in the body of a young man, fell to his knees on the cold stone floor of the palace and made his plea. 'Izanami, I was wrong. You gave your life in childbirth yet I was so concerned with my own unhappiness that I showed you no consideration. Truly I was a conceited, superficial, stupid creature. That is why I have cast aside my godly status. Now that I am no longer a god, please, I beg of you, stop killing my wives — not just my wives. Please stop stealing life from a thousand people each day.'

'Have you decided to refrain from building birthing huts?'

'If you are wondering whether I plan to continue taking women to wife then the answer is no. I have been reborn into the body of a nineteen-year-old man and I have married a young woman. I want to live the rest of my life with her, and that is why I have come here to beg your forgiveness.'

'Where did you meet her?' Izanami whispered. Perhaps the fact that Izanaki was now a young man had helped calm her.

'On Umihebi Island. She served as the priestess of the darkness. Yayoi is her name.'

Yayoi was rescued? She was now Izanaki's wife? Tremendous joy welled within me. But just as suddenly I was overcome by doubt. What would this do to Izanami? I stole a glance in her direction, my heart in turmoil. Izanami had said that her suffering was caused by virtue of her being 'the *female* god'. I felt all the more respect for her, but also all the more pity.

But what Izanami said next surprised me. 'What a coincidence. That young woman's mother is here in the

Realm of the Dead. She serves me. How painful it will be to take this young woman's life – even for me.'

Horrified, I started to beg for Yayoi's life, but Izanaki spoke first.

'Izanami, that's why I am here. Please, spare Yayoi. I am no longer a god. One day I, too, will die. Please, have pity.'

'What will you give me in return for Yayoi's life?'

I listened to them converse, my anxiety mounting.

'Isn't it enough that I now have a limit on my lifespan? Please, Izanami, I should like to see you. Won't you show yourself to me?'

'I will if you return to me once again as a god.' Izanami's voice was ice cold.

Izanaki scrutinised the darkness around him. Each movement of his body had the quickness of youth. Suddenly he shouted, 'The torch won't last much longer. I will have to leave soon. Once my light is gone, I won't be able to find my way out – not in my present condition. So, are we not to meet again, Izanami? Not, that is, until I return in death? By then I have no idea how I will look. Let me bid you farewell now, before it is too late.'

Suddenly Izanami drew alongside Izanaki and blew her breath over him. The flame of the pinewood torch sputtered out as suddenly as if it were a flickering candle. The warm, bright light it had cast was gone. And the darkness that ensued seemed all the darker for it.

'What have you done?'

I could hear panic in Izanaki's voice. He pulled a set of lighter flints from inside his robe and struggled to strike the stones together, but without his left hand, it was impossible. After several minutes had passed, he spoke again: 'Izanami, I beg you. Help me light my torch. I cannot see.'

'Why don't you take a tooth from the comb in your hair and light it as you did all those years ago when you beheld my festering corpse?' Izanami chided, her words filled with spite.

'You know I can't do that now. My hair is no longer knotted in a bunch, and I have no comb. I have no means of starting a fire.' Izanaki was growing frustrated.

'So, you're helpless. You really have become human.' Izanami sighed.

'Yes. That's why you must help me, Izanami. If you don't light my torch, I won't be able to leave.' Izanaki's voice was weaker now.

The darkness was a deeper black and so heavily textured you could have sliced it with a sword. Izanami and I watched as Izanaki floundered in the dark, bumping

into the pillars and crawling frantically over the floor.
He could not see us at all. I was terribly upset to watch
his agitation and wondered what Izanami planned to do
next.

'Izanami! Is this how you intend to take your revenge?'
Izanaki shouted angrily.

'This is hardly revenge. But the Realm of the Dead is
no place for living human beings. Once you transformed
yourself into a human, you violated that taboo, as you
did the last time you visited me here. In all things you
think only of yourself. And you have no qualms about
disrupting order in other worlds. You are now a wayward
human, and I – as a god – am meting out punishment.
That is all.'

According to Izanami, she was punishing him, not
avenging herself. I spoke up in desperation. 'Izanami-
sama, Izanaki-sama has already made his choice. He
has become a human man with a fixed lifespan. He is
also my daughter's husband. I beg you, please, forgive
him.'

Izanami laughed under her breath. 'He still does not
know what it means to be alive. What better time than
now to teach him?'

'But . . .'

Izanami sharply rebuffed any further argument. 'If you

intend to continue pleading his case, then why don't *you* help him, Namima? After all, weren't you eager to take on the tasks of the goddess? Spare his life.'

'I cannot.'

'Why not?' Izanami's entire body was glowing blue and she bore down on me with a terrifying expression. 'Why?'

I managed to answer with a quivering voice. 'Because I'm just an ordinary *human* spirit.'

'And may you never again attempt to do the work of the gods.'

Human beings and gods are different. I now understood how frightening the anger of a god could be. I threw myself on the floor at Izanami's feet. That was all I could do.

'Izanaki, I will take your life and in exchange spare Yayoi.' Izanami spoke with stern authority.

Hearing that Yayoi was safe brought me great relief, yet I could not help but feel sorry for Izanaki – his was such a cruel fate. I remained with my face pressed to the floor, saying nothing. How merciless a goddess Izanami was! I suppose I still did not understand that the intensity of her anger was matched by the depth of her sorrow. Meanwhile Izanaki, terrified of the darkness, had pushed deeper and deeper into the underground realm, all the while weeping and wailing. Izanami made no move to help him. Rather, she followed, watching him silently. Other spirits were also drawn to Izanaki and pressed around him with a soft rustle. Time passed. Izanaki came to a halt and sat on his haunches in the darkness as though resigned to his fate.

After a number of days, he entered a dark crypt at the end of a blind alley where he collapsed on his side. His eyes were open wide in the pitch darkness and he seemed to be struggling for breath. He had had nothing to drink and nothing to eat. It would not be long before he lost the strength to live. He lay on the ground, face down. At the very least I did not want his last hours to be painful, so I came up behind him and wrapped him in my embrace. As soon as I did, I felt something entirely unexpected: Mahito was behind me, propping me up. I could not feel the press of his flesh. Neither could I share his touch. We were mere spirits, after all. But I remembered the happiness I had felt on the boat so long ago. I had been cradling little Yayoi in my arms and Mahito had held me from behind. And now here we were, Mahito and I, holding the man who loved our Yayoi. Weren't we clinging to him, gently restraining him, as we would our own child? I felt something cold trickle down my cheek. I was crying.

'Mahito . . . don't you remember the boat? Don't you remember me? Namima.'

Without thinking, I turned to look at him.

'Namima,' he whispered, and that was all.

'We spent any number of nights just like this aboard that tiny boat. I held our newborn Yayoi, and you held me.'

'I remember some of it. You said you were feeling uneasy and then you died. But it was so long ago. It feels like something that happened before I was born. It feels like something I dreamt.'

'But you killed me! Why did you do it?'

'You're wrong,' Mahito whispered.

I had no idea what to believe, what was true. And yet here, on my back – though I was nothing more than a wraith – I could feel the warmth of Mahito's body. Compared to Izanami, I was still human through and through.

Mahito and I were not the only ones trying to offer Izanaki support. The crypt in which he lay teemed with spirits, those that retained the appearance they had had while alive and those that had been spirits from the very beginning. They all watched over Izanaki.

Izanami left her chamber and, entering the crypt, stood before the dying Izanaki.

'Izanaki, it seems you have reached the end of your
life. I will be waiting for you here in the Realm of the
Dead. Those who die with unresolved desires, those who
are unable to cross over, they join me here in this underground world. Soon you will be here too and we will be
joined again, finally.'

Once she had spoken, Izanaki smiled faintly in the
darkness. His breath was laboured but he managed to
say, 'My beloved Izanami. I will die without regret. I
accepted everything that came my way and lived life
to the fullest. But I have had enough of life. Throughout
the years I had the pleasure of so many exceptional
women – of loving them and being loved. And, Izanami,
I count you among them. Now it will make me very
happy if I can experience death as well. Because I will
know at last what you underwent. And I wonder,
Izanami, are any of those women here? The women I
loved? I doubt it. I doubt that any of them died with
the kind of unresolved desire that would have kept
them tethered here.'

'Oh? Then what of me, Izanaki? Are you suggesting
that I rebuffed all that came my way? For I, too, accepted
everything, every challenge, yet I ended here. Is it my
lot to continue this defiled existence?'

Izanami was clearly angry. Izanaki, unable to see,

turned in the direction of her voice. 'You are a female god. Of course you are not defiled. Rebuff your fate, and henceforth save the spirits here who are unable to float free of their desires? Save them one by one and surely something will be born from it . . . new life.'

'Izanaki, you are naïve.' Izanami laughed shrilly. 'Save your flattery. My defilement bothers me not in the least, and I have no interest in saving anyone! All who end up here will stay here forever, doomed to drift, directionless. How could any good be born of their tiresome grumblings? Please, Izanaki, enough of your childish sentiment! It is my lot, my *choice* to accept all of the world's defilement. And should one delve deeper and deeper still into the heart of this defilement, one might discover there something entirely unexpected. But, Izanaki, that has nothing to do with you.'

'My beloved Izanami, you are strong.' Izanaki laughed quietly. He let out a deep sigh and then he died. His corpse remained as it was for a time in the darkness but then, like melting snow, it slowly disappeared. Perhaps he had moved on to the realm for those who die with no regrets. We spirits, unable to shed real tears, wept in our hearts. We mourned Izanaki, the valiant god we had lost. But we also mourned Izanami for, despite the awesome authority she manifested, she had loved Izanaki deeply. And now the two were finally and irrevocably separated.

For a long time Izanami stared at the surrounding emptiness into which Izanaki had disappeared. And then, finally, she spoke.

'Namima, it is time to attend to our tasks.'

'Izanami-sama, do you still intend to select death for a thousand people, even now that Izanaki-sama has died?' I saw no reason for her to continue.

Izanami's answer took me by surprise. 'I have defeated Izanaki. He was bested by the pain of mourning. But I have no intention of changing my destiny. I am the goddess who metes out death, after all. I will continue.'

Once Izanami had had her say, she set off towards the map room. I hesitated, uncertain what to do. Izanami turned. 'Namima, has your bitterness disappeared?'

'I don't know. And yours, Izanami-sama?'

'It is not something that can ever disappear. But those who extol the joys of living can never understand the feelings of someone forced into the Realm of the Dead. I will continue to hate and abhor and kill for all eternity.'

Izanami's body emitted the pale bluish glow of her

bitterness. She was furious with Izanaki for his ability to become human, and once I recognised this, I was nearly frozen with fear. Izanami – over the long years that she had handed out death – had become a true goddess, and not just that: the quintessential destroyer. But now that Izanaki was dead, surely the regeneration of life would fall to her as well. She was the goddess who invited our desire and also our defilement; she bore the weight of the past and lived on into the future for ever. The realisation filled me with overwhelming awe.

'Izanami-sama, please allow me to serve by your side.'

This, then, is Izanami's story. She serves as the goddess of the Realm of the Dead, now and for ever more. And all around her the grumbling of the restless spirits knows no end but grows and grows and grows. This, too, is beautiful and clear and as insubstantial as dust. Contrary to what Izanaki-sama said just before he died, nothing is born here. And so Izanami continues, without change, to decide the deaths of a thousand people a day.

And I, who was once the priestess of the darkness, feel that serving here at Izanami's side I am able to accomplish what I was unable to finish on earth. For, as I said earlier, Izanami is without doubt a woman among women. The trials that she has borne are the trials all women must face.

Revere the goddess!

In the darkness of the underground palace, I secretly sing her praises.

Sources

Dentô Bunkazai Kiroku Hozonkai/Zaidan hôjin Shimonaka kinen zaidan seisaku (Traditional Cultural Properties Preservation Society Records/A Shimonaka Memorial Foundation Production). *Okinawa Kudakajima no Izaiho* (The Izaiho: Inauguration Rites of Kudakajima Island, Okinawa). Tokyo Shinema shinsha.

Hashimoto Osamu. *Hashimoto Osamu no Kojiki* (Osamu Hashimoto's Kojiki). Kôdansha.

Higa Yasuo. *Nihonjin no tamashi no genkyô Okinawa Kudakajima* (The Birthplace of the Japanese Soul: Kudakajima Island, Okinawa). Shûeisha shinsho.

Miura Sukeyuki. *Kôgoyaku Kojiki kanzenban* (The Modern Language Kojiki, Complete Edition). Bungei shunjû.

Saigô Nobutsuna. *Kojiki chûshaku* (The Annotated Kojiki). Chikuma gakugei bunko.

Saigô Nobutsuna. *Kojiki kenkyû* (Kojiki Studies). Miraisha.

Saigô Nobutsuna. *Kojiki no sekai* (The World of the Kojiki). Iwanami shinsho.

Suzuki Miekichi. *Shinpan Kojiki monogatari* (Kojiki Tales: New Edition). Kadokawa Sofia bunko.

Umehara Takeshi. *Tennôke no "furusato": Hyûga o yuku* (A Tour of Hyûga: The Homeland of the Imperial Family). Shinchô bunko.

Wakugami, Motoo. *Okinawa Kudakajima no Izaiho* (The Izaiho: Inauguration Rites of Kudakajima Island, Okinawa). Sunagoya shobô.

The translator consulted the following:
Kojiki. Translated with an introduction and notes by Donald L. Philippi. Tokyo: University of Tokyo Press, 1968.